Southern Breeze & Mimosa Trees

Kate Montgomery

Magnolia Manuscripts Press

DEDICATION

To my husband for endlessly cheering me on when the nights got late, and I felt overwhelmed. Thanks for always being my biggest cheerleader.

Chapter One

♥

-Greer-

The sound of the screen door closing and the smell of coffee. To me, this is how every morning should start. I can feel the early morning heat, with the promise of more to come, and the slightly flat cushions on the porch furniture. And it feels like pure bliss. Unfortunately, I don't get to wake up like that many days. Instead, I hear traffic and alarm clocks. But at least there is the smell of coffee. Today, it is what gets me out of bed. Thank God for coffee.

Last night, my dreams were filled with mimosa trees, summer breezes, and time spent on the porch with my aunt, Hattie. She gave me that space and a place to just be. No pressure. Life has not always been easy, but she made it feel manageable. It has been far too long since we have sat on the porch. I need to go home. Over the last few months, I realized that I am not happy anymore. Life hasn't turned out like I'd planned. Not because I didn't plan. More likely because I've over-planned. Some people feel trapped- living in the city and working a corporate middle-management job they never wanted. Not me; that was exactly what I wanted. The corporate girly life was for me. College at Georgia Tech, followed by my dream internship. Landed a tech job at one of my top 3 firms shortly after that. Gorgeous apartment. I worked that ladder like the boss I'd imagined myself being. Looking at my vision board, I am crushing it. But I am not happy.

Life has felt like clothes that don't fit right anymore. I tried meditation, exercise, and deep breathing and saw a therapist. Then I realized that the thought that keeps circling round and round is that I need to go home. The thoughts finally moved from the back of my mind solidly to the front, and I made my decision. Once I did, it was like my serotonin and dopamine (or whatever they are) turned back on. Suddenly, I was flooded with happiness again. I started taking steps to put my plan into action. I LOVE a good plan.

The first thing to do was to call Hattie. Despite having lived with her for most of my life, I wanted to make sure she was okay with me moving back home. Of course, she was more than on board. Up next was work. My job doesn't require me to be here, and since I'm a workaholic, there were no concerns from their end with me transitioning to working remotely. The final step was giving notice to my apartment complex. I'd waited over a year for this apartment, so finding a new tenant here will be no issue. This place will be snapped up in a heartbeat by another waitlist hopeful. If I were someone who believed in fates or signs, I'd say this was all lining up perfectly, like it was meant to be. All of my pieces are falling into place. Instead, I'll say I'm immensely grateful. I get to go home!

-Hattie-

The porch has always been my favorite place in the house. When Davis and I bought this place, the porch sold us. We knew we'd be out here every day, and we were. Mornings started with coffee, dogs, and spending time together outside. Not doing, just being. Time passes so quickly that it feels like it was just yesterday but also like it really was over 30 years ago.

It's been over five years since my last morning coffee with Davis. Every morning that I am out here, there's bitter mixed in with the sweet. I choose to focus on how much he loved being out here instead of the fact that he isn't here. Isn't that what most of life is: choosing how we see things?

Enough of my dwelling in the past, I got the best news I've had in a long time! My sweet girl, Greer, is coming home. It has been months (8 if we're keeping track) since she was able to sneak away from work in Atlanta to come stay. This news was even better than a visit; she's moving home! I tried to hide how excited I was and managed to hide my tears until after the call. She has no idea how much this means to have her here. It's the breath of fresh air we all need.

Meg and I talked right after and started immediately planning what all we need to do. Heavy emphasis on the WE. I started a mile-long list and included a surprise welcome-home BBQ. We'll see if we can pull off the surprise. The to-do list is circling, the dogs are barking, and my coffee is cooling time to get busy. But for now, I'm going to take a minute to savor my time on the porch and reflect on why I'm feeling so grateful for all these changes.

–Meg–

I hear Hattie's dogs cheerfully barking and know she's on the porch. It makes me smile. After Davis died, the porch mornings were hard for her, and it took her a while to find her peace there again. So, each day she's out, there brings me joy. Hattie and her porch have been a space that many of us have sought refuge in over the years. Seeing her love for porch mornings grow back felt like balance returning to our little corner of the world.

I've lived next to Hattie and Davis for more than twenty years. I moved in as a starry-eyed newlywed and now reside as a slightly salty, mostly happy divorced mom with twin teenagers. In the last two decades, I have desperately needed those chats with Hattie to keep my sanity. My kiddos have found friendship and learned that family doesn't have to be blood.

This week, our plan for Greer's return kicks into high gear. Time to pour a cup and head over!

-Erin-

Running a coffee shop and helping with my husband's construction company does not leave me with loads of free time. What I do have is sprinkled between family and friends. My husband Calvin (Cal) is gone more than I am, so when we're home, it is like the stars have aligned. Our boys are grown and mostly gone. Eddie and his wife, Kayla, have the most precious baby girl, Annie, who is the absolute light of our lives. Max is gone with his dad at work on jobs most days or along the coast somewhere when he isn't working. Seraphina just got engaged and is in the throes of wedding planning, even though we're a year out. Lauren is on break from college and is planning her great adventure to the Keys for a month with a group of girlfriends. Like I said, I am sprinkled amongst them when I can find one of them.

Otherwise, I am with my old lady gang, as my girls refer to it. Annabelle (Greer's mama), Hattie, and I had been thick as thieves since kindergarten. We felt more like sisters than friends. In that way, Greer feels like my niece, too.

Along the way, we've added others to our group, and we stick together like glue. We could not be more excited for Greer's homecoming. She needed to have her time and space to be her own person. Her life has not been easy or smooth. But she's always had Hattie and most of us. Coming home by her own choice feels right in so many ways, and her timing is perfect.

-Sylvie-

My husband Ben and I relocated from Miami 15 years ago. We'd tired of the "big city" life and dreamt of opening a thrift or secondhand shop in a coastal town. It always felt like a pipe dream. While on a weekend trip, we'd seen some open spaces and called a realtor. That's how we met Davis Thatcher. Ben and Davis hit it off immediately. It was like they'd been friends since childhood. Davis insisted I'd love Hattie, and he was right. While our personalities are vastly different, we got along just like he thought we would. Traditionally, I didn't make friends easily, but with Hattie, it was easy. She made it feel simple.

Chapter Two

♥

-Greer-

Packing is likely my least favorite activity, especially when I have had to sacrifice vacation days for it. It has to get done, though. As I stand here looking around, all I can think is, where did all of this crap come from, and how did it fit in here?!?

I am a self-proclaimed packrat. Not like a hoarder, more of a memory collector. Unfortunately, those memories often come with a tangible item that I end up stashed in a box or a plastic bin for later. Rarely to ever been seen again. All those little bits of paper and scraps of things. It's hard sometimes to decide what should stay and what should go. Other times, it is easy- especially when I have no idea why I've kept it. Ticket stubs from concerts as a teenager, plane tickets from trips with friends, pressed flowers from old boyfriends. All sweet, but to what end? Am I keeping it because I feel like I should or because I really am attached? I did get teary over a poem from a friend, and I am definitely saving that one. The rest can be pitched.

One thing that makes packing easier is good music. Hosting a high-volume solo karaoke all-day session has helped me shake off all those sappy moments. The gallon of iced coffee hasn't hurt either. Normally I am a hot coffee gal, but cleaning, errands, and apparently now, packing call for iced coffee. Honestly, hoping that packing does not become a routine part of my life; this is enough for a while.

I am a creature of habit and enjoy routine. Throwing caution to the wind is not my style. Giving up what I spent more than a decade working on shows how desperately this change is needed. I am willing to shift my entire routine (admittedly, it is boring) and go back home. My aunt's home and life are not structured like mine. It's something I find comforting, nerve-wracking, exciting, and normal, all in one chaotic set of emotions.

My last move was from my first big girl apartment to this one. Six years ago, with no real big emotions other than self-congratulations, it was a well-deserved upgrade from the other apartment I had been in. After my last promotion and pay bump, I'd decided that I deserved to go on the year-plus waitlist for this corner unit looking over the park. This move conjures an entirely different set of emotions. I was not prepared for them either. I did not have them on my checklist, which makes me giggle and also makes me sound like I need to revisit that therapist. Also, very glad I did not go so far as making my planned spreadsheet of room-by-room tasks. Grateful that I'd run out of time for that one...haha. Dare I add "relax" to my to-do list? Maybe just mentally. And perhaps have less coffee and a glass of water.....I'm getting a little batty.

The next thing I realize, the sun is setting, and I have made major progress. The living room, dining room, and linen closet are completely packed. Go me! Time for dinner, and I know exactly what I want. There's a local pizza place that I know I'll miss. So, patio pizza and wine sounds like an ideal plan. My thoughts turn to the company at dinner. Is there someone I want to join? The sad reality is that there honestly isn't. I've got a few girls I am friendly with from work and church.

No one that I want to or even feel comfortable calling up to hang out with for a last-minute dinner.

At this moment, I realize I am painting a bleak picture of my social life, but it really isn't that bad. Mostly, I am focused on work and do go out for the occasional dinner or girls' night. There have been boyfriends that have come and gone. James and I were together for almost three years and talked about getting married. His surprise interest in strippers ended things suddenly, though. After that fireball ending, sticking with my "normal" friends from back home feels easier. Looking forward to rekindling those relationships and building stronger ones. Yikes! Who knew moving was this therapeutic? My pizza and wine are in progress, I am calling it for the night and heading to bed straight after this.

How quickly days pass when spent endlessly wrapping, taping, and packing into boxes! It feels like hours, but my achy back reminds me of the actual timeframe. Despite my pizza reflections from a few days ago, I did have a meet-up with a couple of friends to say farewells. I'm only moving a few hours away, but to friends in the city that can feel like states away. When your days, and many evenings, are consumed by work, the idea of driving out to the coast for a day or two can feel ridiculous. I completely understand because I've had those phases. I'm definitely in a space to be out there full-time now. Counting the hours (not even days anymore) until the moving truck comes!

Made the decision this week to sell the majority of my furniture. It represents a time, place, and a look I was attempting to go for. City chic isn't my vibe, but I thought it went with the look of the apartment. I'll honestly be glad to be rid of the hard furniture. None of it would blend in at Hattie's, either. She and I share a similar vintage coastal aesthetic. Not in a tacky, campy way, but in a classic vintage way.

While I won't have furniture, I will have approximately one thousand boxes of stuff to put away. Can't even remember if there's a storage place near the house. Of all the things to have left off my list, that's a doozy. Taking a few seconds, I quickly search for storage facilities and find several nearby. Snagging screenshots is the easiest way to pick a few to save them to call later.

The furniture has nearly all sold, the boxes are in neat rows. Trash is taken out and I'm about to hop into the car. Cannot believe I'm finally ready to go. Only way to describe how I am feeling is when you're at the top of a roller coaster and about to drop over that first hill. The fun is about to start, your brain is flooded with happy emotions, but you have that little thrill of fear too. That's me right now as I'm getting into the car. Let the fun begin! I am so ready.

-Hattie-

Pacing myself has never been one of my strongest gifts. Sadly, I've had to learn how to over the last few weeks. Getting the house ready for Greer to come home has been the most joyful thing though. It has been a long while since I've had something like this to look forward to and this is just what the doctor ordered, quite literally. A refresh of things has been in order for some time around here anyway. I am blessed to have an army of supportive friends who are willing and able to assist. Everything came together so quickly. I cannot wait for her to see it!

Greer's childhood bedroom has a girlish charm that is no longer fit for a woman in her 30s. Part of me wanted to paper over it, but the soft yellow wallpaper with dainty pink and white flowers is too precious to me, and I can't do it. Instead, we shuffled some of the rooms around and made that into an office space for her as a surprise. It has the best lighting for all of those online meetings she has all the time. For her bedroom, we cleaned out one of the larger bedrooms upstairs. Even though it doesn't have an attached bathroom, I'm hoping she'll be pleased with the larger closets and more floor space.

When I say, "cleaned out", I don't want you to take this lightly. These rooms had gotten messy and out of control. They'd turned into a dumping ground for items we weren't sure what to do with it. Why does it all stack up so easily? Could have easily furnished my first apartment with all the clutter in those two rooms. It was largely able to be donated, or as Greer would say "donate-able". We'd put out the call to see if anyone we knew needed anything, but most went to Sylvie and Ben's shop.

The cleanout was long overdue, I had MY grand-mother's dishes. She's been gone for well over fifty years and they've not been used for over twenty. While I've loved them since childhood, it is time to give some-one else a chance. There were things I couldn't bring myself to part with. Most of those belonged to Davis or Annabelle. They're safely stashed away in our office. Shortly after Davis died, we went through and donated what I could bear. But what remains is what I trea-sure. So, it stays and will likely stay until Greer has to deal with it when I'm dead and gone. Very few of those items were in the guest rooms, most were in our bedroom or office.

I made the decision early on to keep Davis's office intact. It was really more of our shared space we both worked from. It just felt right to keep it. Over time, the room became a library of sorts with shelves and shelves of our favorite books. It just feels like Davis, when I close my eyes, I can see him leaned forward on the desk, intently focused on a task or a book. On a chilly night, I still like to build a fire and snuggle up with a book and the dogs in there. I miss him a little bit less on those nights.

After the cleaning and organizing, the actual fun started. We got down to work planning the refresh of the bathroom and bedrooms. Redecorating is one of my favorite things in life and Greer had given me carte blanche. It works out perfectly that our styles match so well. She's been trying this city chic look that doesn't suit her in the most recent apartment. When we discussed her homecoming, one of our topics was her need for new furniture. She couldn't wait to get rid of what she had- couch, chairs, tables, and even her bedroom set. We agreed that we're coastal people. All that leather and sharp edges doesn't cut it.

A little bit is fine, but we need to balance it out with softness. You've got to bring the colors and textures of the outside in. Meg, Erin, Sylvie and I have spent the last couple of weeks finding just the right pieces to match with linens. Blending the old and the new putting it all together has brought me so much joy! Now, I'm itching to keep going with a few other rooms in the house. Sylvie and I have gone through their store with my wish list and she knows all the extra pieces I'm on the lookout for to add to the house.

Cannot wait to see her face when she gets here! Hoping the updated rooms add to her peace and help her feel like she has a sanctuary. Greer doesn't talk much about her feelings, she never has. For her to ask to come home, to say she needs to come home, says so much. Giving her a safe space to rest will help her open up when she's ready. In her own time, she'll share when it feels right for her.

We've planned a surprise party tonight to welcome Greer home. Nothing extreme- more of a cocktail hour and dinner on the porch. Maybe *hours* is more accurate? Meg and the twins, Sylvie and Ben, Erin, Cal and all their kids plus the grandbaby, and the dogs. My ever-present fleet of dogs, all five of them, adore having company, whenever my friends come their dogs usually do too. The more, the merrier. A night on the porch may rival a morning on the porch depending on who is present. Our little group each has a favorite food or drink to bring. It always comes together easily.

In a few hours, we'll all be settled on the porch with cocktails in hand and surrounded by all our favorite people. Feels absolutely surreal! Like a new chapter is starting, one that I didn't expect or know I needed.

–Meg–

Sarah and Seth are talking non-stop about Greer coming home. She's been their favorite neighbor/babysitter/summer playmate for most of their lives. Her going away to the city was so sad for them. Their little hearts didn't realize that Greer isn't really family or a permanent part of the neighborhood. Despite being in their "cool" teenage years, they're obviously excited and I find it beyond precious. Both keep asking me what I think Greer will think about things–books, music, video games. It crushes my heart because I only now see how much they've been missing her, and I haven't noticed. Mom guilt will always find a way to rear its head. Why is it like that? My beautiful kids are happy to see a friend they've missed, and my brain makes me feel guilty about it. Ugh!

We've been helping Hattie get the house ready for Greer's homecoming. She's been de-cluttering, paint-ing, decorating- basically working any spare hour she has. Not that the house needed much, but her utter delight in Greer's return has prompted a full-scape update. In Hattie's mind, the house was a disaster and required a major overhaul. Even went so far as to redo some of the already impeccable landscaping. Hattie knows Greer loves the smell of Gardenias and Jasmine, so she's added a few extra of each.

Greer is as close to her own child as Hattie has come. She would do anything to make that girl happy. Some might think that planting a few extra fragrant plants is too much or a tad silly. I can guarantee that neither of them would view it that way. Their thought? "I am immensely grateful" and said with sincerity. One of these days, I need to ask where that phrase comes from. They say it a lot, and I've even caught myself using it but don't know the background.

Hattie is somewhere in her 50s. As close as I can add up, she's in the later part. She is always vague and says "in my 50s" but that is all the commitment I can get. Erin is in on it and just gives a conspiratorial smile.

Both of them still act like they're in their 30s. Not that 50s are elderly and for the most part, Hattie has the energy of someone half her age. Throughout the last three weeks, she has worked until the wee hours taking on tasks. Erin, Sylvie, and I have helped as much as we can and we'll leave completely exhausted. When we check in the next morning, Hattie will already be at work or at the least out on the porch, working on her plan for the day.

The party tonight will be the cherry on top for all of us! I am genuinely looking forward to reconnecting with Greer as an adult. We aren't that far apart in age, it felt like we were when she was younger but in reality, we're far closer than Hattie and I are. Our relationship has mostly been my friendship with her aunt and knowing her as a teen. It will be so nice to get to know her as an adult and her own person. Welcoming her into our circle is going to be so fun!

Each of us preps for a night on the porch at Hattie's in our own way. Summer salads are one of my favorites, for tonight I'm going peach caprese with local produce and olive oil. Serving with a side of toasty baguettes. Drooling just thinking about it! Sarah has recently started to make her own contributions. She and her friends have decided to learn how to bake and she's planning to make her first ever key lime pie. Seth is interested in helping tonight too. He texted Cal and asked if he can help grill. He's never asked before, so this is a huge step. I am doing my best to stay cool about it, probably not succeeding.

Feels like we're entering a new phase. Lately, I've been reminding myself that my friends aren't necessarily their friends. Adjusting my view seems to have the potential for a positive change. It has taken the twins quite a while to want to be involved. Sure, they came along with me and were content to spend time with everyone. But asking to be involved is a big step.

I wish I could say that I have given them time and space and didn't force them to go. But that would be a giant lie. After their dad left, it was just us. Too much had happened in a short span of time; we closed ranks for a bit, and I did forced family fun time. To see them now participating by choice boggles my mind. Parenting is always a back and forth of what was working doesn't anymore, so for now we'll just celebrate their happiness to join in. I will keep trying to act natural about it while I do a happy dance in my head and cry about it over lunches with my friends later. We have to get a move on to be ready in time for tonight.

Chapter Three

♥

-Greer-

Pulling into the circular driveway at Hattie's feels like a weight is lifting off my chest and shoulders. Simultaneously an ending and a beginning. Is that what beginning "a new chapter" feels like? It's been eight months since I was home, which is the longest since my junior year of college. The majority of my childhood was spent here with my mother. We spent so much time at my Uncle and Aunt's house that it has always felt like my true home, no matter where else we lived. As time passed, the four of us began referring to it as "our" house. In childhood, you don't recognize the dynamics in the background. All I knew was this was a place of love and safety. Other houses may have felt stressful, but the beach house never was.

After my mom purchased our own home nearby, we still spent a lot of time here. We would pop over for dinner on the porch, get togethers with Erin, Cal, and Meg. Every weekend we would have dinner at least one night. In the summers, Davis and Hattie would host movie nights in the yard for the kids while all the adults spent time playing cards and sharing stories. We spent so much time at the house as a family.

For context, my mom and Uncle Davis are siblings. He was a few years older and fell pretty hard for her best friend, Hattie when he came home from college. She and Uncle Davis married the year before I was born. My parents, Annabelle and Joel, were high school sweethearts. They married at eighteen, I was born when they were almost twenty. They split up when I was two and were officially divorced when they were twenty-four. During the divorce, Mom and I moved in with my uncle and aunt and we stayed for quite a while. Joel (I struggle to call him Dad since he wasn't really around) remarried within a couple years of the divorce, I'm fuzzy on the timeline but thinking I may have been in kindergarten or first grade. He has been happily married to Janine and living in Idaho for decades. I bear them no ill will and have, at times, spent vacations with them. We stay in touch, and I keep them up on all my major life events. Janine and I talk more than Joel and I. Over the years, I've tried to have a better relationship with Joel, having now come to the conclusion that we are friendly but never close.

When I was fifteen, Mom was diagnosed and died quickly from an aggressive form of breast cancer. From diagnosis to death, she was only sick for about nine months. Rather than disrupt my life more than it already was, before she died my parents gave Davis and Hattie guardianship of me. I spent my remaining teen years here instead of relocating to Idaho. I don't know how I would have come out of it if the circumstances had been different. It was one of the hardest times of my life. This is my deep connection to Hattie, Davis, and this house. It wasn't just the house that was home, it was the people. Cannot believe I am back and beginning an adult chapter here. So ready to begin again!

Tears are stinging at my eyes while I struggle with my seatbelt. At first, I'd thought it was sweat that had run down my face. Georgia humidity is no joke and will have you sweating without realizing it. Throughout my life, I have not been a big crier, tears don't come easily. But the last few weeks have been a new territory for me. I am happier in this moment than I have been in a long while, so the tears just simply shock. Sheesh– I was not prepared for there to be so many emotions with moving.

After I free myself from the seatbelt, I finally get the door open. Spending the last several hours in air conditioning has not primed me for the warm, wet air. It feels like opening a steamy oven. Not city humid air either, this has the sting of salty sea air. My God, I've missed that smell. The sensation of it building up on your skin when you've been out for a while. The house sits miles from the beach but is close enough to surround you with the tangy, salty southern breeze. I love it so much.

A chorus of dogs barking erupts. Instantly my tears are replaced by an ear-to-ear grin. The kind that makes you feel like your lips might crack. The dogs mean Hattie is nearby. Dev, the smallest and youngest, makes it to me first. He launches himself into my arms, I swear that dog can fly. Pete, Reno, and Ella reach me right after and surround me all at once. Jumping, licking, barking. Sadie lumbers from the house in her gentle way, giving me soft woofs as a greet- ing. Once she's finally by my side, she leans hard into my legs. Every time I am greeted by the dogs, their lev- els of excitement crack me up. It's as if their excitement is governed by their size. We've got the whole spectrum from Sadie's quiet leaning that is reassuring, to Dev wriggling and practically screeching with joy.

Over the dogs, I hear Hattie's voice call out, "Ok, now it's my turn." At the sound of her voice, the dogs gleefully run to join her (well, Sadie doesn't run) as she walks toward me. She makes a beeline for me, and suddenly, I'm enveloped in a hug that soothes me to my bones. We're both laughing and talking at the same time, asking questions and answering in a continuous stream.

Hattie has my sweaty, tear-stained face in her hands and is staring at me. Her enormous smile matches my own, she is beaming, and I am so happy to see her again. However, unlike me, she is not a sweaty mess and remains the picture of southern elegance. She is dressed in pale pink linen capris, a sleeveless tropical print top, with sparkling sandals. Hattie dresses daily like she has somewhere to be, and I have always been in awe of it. An opposite of that, I'm usually in a hurry to get ready for the day. Maybe being here, I'll learn a lesson or two? It hasn't stuck yet but this time it will.

We make our way to the house, arm in arm, sur-rounded by our canine escorts. Crossing into the cool house, I pause for a second before closing the door. I lean against it and smile once again. Could there have been a more perfect welcome home?

We sit in the kitchen for a few minutes and then ultimately decide to catch up out on the porch. No matter the heat, there is a lovely breeze today that knocks the temperature down. Neither of us minds heat or humidity. Mom used to tease us about our shared enjoyment of "basting" in the sun. It simply does not seem to bother us, or rather to deter us. The salty warm air energizes me after the long drive out.

I take a few minutes to wander around the yard with the dogs, noticing the landscaping. Sniffing the fragrant gardenias, a favorite of mine. It might be my imagination, but it feels like there are more than there used to be. I love seeing all the beautiful white blossoms. The climbing jasmine, saw palmettos and fluffy pink mimosa trees are all around the property. Hattie has always taken such pride in this yard. With a final throw of the ball and a deep inhale of the warm air, I take the porch steps two at a time to sit with Hattie. On my way up, I comment on how beautiful the garden is and how much I've missed it. She responds with an appreciative smile.

We spend the next hour or so getting caught up briefly on the happenings of the last few weeks. I can't help but notice that Hattie seems slightly more tired than usual. She runs circles around me and is typically doing small tasks around the porch and in the yard even when resting. The woman does not sit still well. Today, she's happy to sit with her sweet tea and chat. Hearing all the fun she's been up to lately, I can easily see why she'd be tired. Trips to Savannah and Charleston for the day. Erin even convinced her to run to St. Augustine for a quick trip to visit a new coffee supplier. They'd turned it into a girl's weekend and found a few new fun food and shopping spots. Hattie has turned into quite the adventurer lately. We start talking about trips we should take through the summer and fall. Before we forget, I start a list on my phone; this is all too exciting. We are like teenagers planning a school break.

Hattie checks her watch and asks if I'd like help grabbing anything from the car. We're creeping up on dinner and I'm hoping we can grill tonight and eat outside. In the last few years, I've eaten too many meals inside. Barring a rainstorm, Hattie will side with eating outdoors, so that was an easy win.

The "few" things I was bringing turned into a haul when I was packing the car. I'm realizing that it is going to take me more than a couple of trips in and out to get a good start on it. The cargo area in my SUV made it too easy to overload the car with alleged essentials until the moving truck comes in a few days. I question my sanity as I mentally review everything I brought with me.

I head out to grab my first load while Hattie offers to run interference with the pups. While they're absolute loves, they're also absolute trip hazards on the stairs when you're surrounded. I decide to bring in my overnight bag, gym bag, shoes, and my work bag to get started. Leaving my laptop to roast in the humid car does not seem ideal. Anything beyond true essentials and food can wait for now. The heat and humidity while carrying loads of stuff in and out will catch up to me quickly. I need to strategize how to avoid this taking more than two trips.

Struggling up the steps and onto the landing. I spy Hattie grinning like a fairytale cat with a story to tell. Her hand rests on my bedroom door. I blow my damp hair off my sweaty forehead and eye her suspiciously. She definitely has something she's dying to show me.

"What's up Hattie? You look like you can barely contain yourself." She quietly laughs instead of responding. As I reach my door, she shakes her head and points to the next door. I raise an eyebrow to ask "huh?"

She says, "Open it, and you'll see." Now I'm nervous-excited. We'd talked about some projects she had going on, but I wasn't given any specifics.

I open the door to the guest room and gasp. Not being dramatic at all in the description, I actually gasped out loud and am left with my mouth gaping wide open. The guest room is stunning! It was always a beautiful room, but Hattie truly transformed it. For years there has been a soft mint green wall color with toile curtains and linens depicting a French pastoral scene. All anchored together with a vintage bamboo bedroom set. The room felt breezy and cool, like a glass of water with cucumber and mint.

The bamboo furniture remains. The set has been rearranged to catch the morning sun and allow breeze to blow directly over the foot of the bed. Never pictured the room laid out this way, and it works so well! A pale blue-green color has replaced the mint green. The walls now glow with the hue of a perfect piece of sea glass. A textured jute rug fills the center of the room. Luxurious white and cream linens and pillows are piled high on the bed. Toss pillows and a patterned throw bring the colors together. One corner of the room now has a small seating area with a chair, ottoman, and side table. Along the wall above the dresser is a large painting, it fills the space with colors of the sea and sky. The painting feels familiar, but I can't place it in this moment. Small porthole style mirrors are arranged above the bed and reflect the natural light all through the room.

Hattie softly chuckling breaks my gawking around the room. Clearly, she can tell how delighted I am.

"How in the world did you get all of this done?" I ask.

"All with the help of friends" she responds, still smiling, "They were more than willing to jump in. Recognize anything in here?"

"Other than the furniture everything seems new. There is something about that painting that is familiar, but I can't place it."

"It's Max's work!" she chirps, and I can hear the pride in her voice.

"No way! The last of his works I saw were all small-scale pieces. This is massive and the colors are phenomenal." The painting truly is a work of art. Abstract with colors of the sea that blend in and out of one another. It creates the feeling of standing on the beach on a misty morning. I am seriously impressed. Max's work has always been beautiful and ethereal, this has that same feeling, but it seems like it was made for this space.

"Erin and Cal are so proud. He's spent the last year having a few gallery shows and events up and down the coast. I bought this one during his show opener here a few months ago. I'd had him keep it on the wall in the studio until I found the right space for it."

I take a few more seconds to take the room in. Cannot believe this is the same space from late last year. Hattie's got some serious skills.

"Enough gawping, we've got more to see. Put those bags down and follow me", Hattie says as she spins on her heel and heads out of the room. I quickly put my bags on the floor and follow into the hallway. She swings open the door to the guest bath. It has been similarly transformed from a lovely space to a magazine-worthy room. Like the bedroom, the coastal colors bring some of nature into the space. There are sea glass and bamboo accents pulled in to make the rooms have a shared theme. Not in a kitschy way, but in a fresh earthy way.

While I'm complimenting Hattie on her transformations, I catch the twinkle in her eye. Which tells me there may be more to come. I don't want to seem ungrateful, but I cannot help but ask in a stage whisper, "Is there more?"

Back out the door we go! On the other side of the hall-way, my former bedroom door is cracked open slightly. Without asking, I make my way to the door. While the soft yellow wallpaper has stayed. The rest of the room has been reconfigured into a work-from-home paradise. Things I would never have thought of- a mini fridge and coffee bar, a standing desk with a ring light. She thought of major needs, nice to haves, and made them all happen. Executed it all flawlessly and didn't say a word about it!

"Hattie! I am in awe. Always knew you had a love of decorating. Can't believe how much you got done in such a short span of time."

"It was overdue, and I thought there wouldn't be a more perfect time. Since we are getting a fresh start, why not let the house have one too?"

This time I am not surprised when tears spring up. We grab one another in a hug and say, "I'm so happy!" at the same time. Which makes all the dogs bark and us laugh even more.

A long hot shower and change of clothes later and I am back in the kitchen with Hattie. She's mid-cocktail prep on a large batch of coconut mojitos. From the fridge, I grab the sweet tea and pour two glasses. As I am reaching for some of the fresh mint on the counter, the doorbell rings. Hattie looks at me with one eyebrow raised. I take that as my cue to head for the door.

Accompanied by a fleet of very excited dogs, I half jog down the hallway to the door with a quick shout of "coming" for whoever is on the other side of the door. We aren't expecting anyone that I know of. The beauty of Hattie's is that at any point, you could be having company. Dinner for two becomes a dinner for six at the drop of a hat. The dogs all patiently wait for me to catch up and open the door. A hint that they know who it is.

I whip the door open and stare for a second before shrieking, "No way!" into the porch full of people I love most in the world. They all shout "SURPRISE!" in unison and then dissolve into laughter. This unleashes chaos as our dogs start barking and greeting everyone.

Hattie appears behind me clapping, very clearly proud of herself. Her face lit up in childlike delight. She's carried off yet another amazing surprise. Other than the gallon of mojitos, I had no idea we might be having company. I just thought it was going to be a night of hefty drinking on the porch to catch up.

From the back of the group, Cal shouts "Let's get this party started!" Only then do I notice the large cooler he and Max are carrying between them. Seth begins clicking tongs in the air like maracas. People and dogs start streaming past me into the house. Extra dogs have joined in the evening of fun. Max brought his lab, Brady. Erin and Cal brought Teensy and Margie. Lauren's Staffy, Blueberry, bulldozes in with a dog that I've never seen before. Seraphina's mega-sized Mastiff, Beefcake, rumbles slowly down the hallway. The dogs bolt through the house and straight to the backdoor. Sarah says, "I'll get 'em" and heads to the door.

In no time, the house is filled with voices. Everyone talking at once. Moving. Laughing. Different things are happening, but it all seems coordinated. Leaning against the doorway, I pause for a moment. Erin squeezes my shoulder as she shimmies past me. Sylvie pats my back on her way to the fridge. Meg hip bumps me walking to the table with a plate of appetizers. Each offering their own welcome home. Hattie catches my eye and smiles warmly. This is the homecoming she wanted me to have.

I pop out onto the deck and help Kayla, Lauren, and Seraphina to get the tables set up and ready. Bonus, it gives us a chance to catch up. Eddie and Kayla's daughter is eight months old and already trying to walk. The last time I was home, Kayla was still pregnant. Wild to think her baby is here and moving around! Lauren is getting ready to sail to the Keys for a month with a group of girlfriends. Seraphina (we've called her Surf most of her life) finished grad school and is recently engaged. As we work together on laying out the table, we start making plans to meet up this coming week for lunch, coffee dates, and walks.

Magically, as soon as the table is laid, food starts appearing. Porch parties are always the most delicious. Everyone contributes something, a blend of repeat favorites and trying out new recipes. The smell of meat wafts up from below the deck. Cal, Max, and Seth are grilling up a drool-inducing variety. By the time we assemble the sides, dips, condiments, and drinks, the meat is being placed in platters on the table. Seth is grinning with pride as the group of us "ooh" and "ahh". Meg had whispered earlier that this was his first time grilling. He looks pleased as punch and it makes me so happy. My heart aches at how grown but innocently sweet this moment has been.

Everyone takes a seat, and food starts passing around the table. The conversations start back up about the day's activities, upcoming plans for the summer, and general family chatter. But as the plates and mouths fill, the chatting drops off. I'm not sure my plate can hold much more. The center is filled with steak bites and grilled shrimp. Around the edges I've piled in tomato salad, a peach caprese salad, coleslaw, mac and cheese, an ear of corn, and a couple of freshly shucked oysters. In a small bowl, there's a side of Brunswick stew with a piece of cornbread. I am one happy, happy gal as I dig in.

Plates empty and conversation springs back to full volume as some add seconds and thirds. Wine and mojitos (sweet tea for the kiddos) make another pass around the table. I notice Ben shifting around. He leans forward and tops off my wine. Once he's satisfied with the amount in the glass, he sits back and puffs his cheeks out with a sigh. Pretty sure he's got loads of questions that he's been itching to ask.

"So, kiddo, what brings you back?" he blurts out.

Sylvie jumps in, "Geez Ben, you can ease into your interrogation!" Which prompts a few giggles around the table.

"Come on now. Greer likes that I'm direct!" he offers as a defense.

This leads to more giggles. While we may not always love it, we do love Ben. It is sort of the same thing.

"To put it simply, it was time. I thought city life and my job were what I needed, or I guess just wanted. The reality hit- it wasn't. The job is still something I love, but the city isn't. Being here is what I need."

"Makes sense to us sweetie. The city has its moment. Then it is time to go find some peace and space to relax." Sylvie responds.

"That's how I have been feeling. The season for it had passed."

Eddie has been listening with intensity, "How long had you been thinking about it?"

"Longer than I consciously realized. It felt cumulative and built incrementally until it was all I could think about. After my last visit home, that's when I really began thinking about it. Canceled trips and work conflicts prevented me from getting back when I wanted to. The idea of mundane things keeping me away was soul-crushing."

Heads nod around the table. All eyes are on me. There's so much more I want to say, more to share. But openly sharing is not in my wheelhouse. If not now, when? I take a few breaths and stare into my wine glass like it is some sort of crystal ball. I suddenly notice that it's now nearly empty.

"I don't make snap decisions, no matter how much I want it. For this, I felt like I needed to be home and had to figure out how to make it happen. Trying to be true to myself, so I made a list to weigh my options (insert everyone uproariously laughing). Briefly, I considered quitting my job completely. Instead, fully remote was the route chosen. And....tada....here I am" I end uncomfortably and use some dorky jazz hands in an effort to reduce my embarrassment.

Erin and Hattie pick up on how uncomfortable I'm feeling. Each begins chatting about all the "new" businesses and activities in town. When I catch their eyes, a quick little kiss is blown as a thank you. In sync, they quickly nod their heads while talking. How can two women who aren't actually related be the same person?

Chairs scrape as Sarah and Meg head toward the house. In a minute they return with a stunning duo of key lime pies. One is topped with a sky-high meringue and the other with whipped cream and lime slices. Sarah is testing out which version is the most popular. This is the perfect diversion, and the conversation switches to which one we're each tasting first and then merges back into general chit-chat.

By 10 p.m., everyone has made their way home. As a group we got most things tidied up. Hattie and I finish a few things, deciding what will wait for us to do tomorrow, ending by prepping the coffee for the morning.

The tea kettles sings to us and we make our way to the porch with herbal tea. It's been a tradition since I was in my teens, the tea helps us sleep. I light our candle and bug torches. The porch is lit in a comforting glow. We take our favorite spots, Hattie on the loveseat with two dogs, me in a rocking chair with a dog, and two on the ottoman. They're worn out from running with the dogs and kids all evening. An hour or so later, we're both bleary-eyed and yawning aggressively. It's been a long and beautiful day. My belly and heart are full. Calling it a night and dragging ourselves upstairs to our beds.

-Hattie-

What a day it has been! Greer's arrival has been a whirlwind. It feels like it's been two full days. Despite my exhaustion, my brain is still busy reliving the day. My heart is happy. It was so refreshing to watch Greer laugh and talk with her people, those who've loved her most of her life. She moves through the house like it's second nature. I'm drawn back to memories of her living here with Davis and me. Many years of wonderful memories all together.

Ending our night with tea and dogs on the porch was a delightful way to wrap up the day. We're on the cusp of summertime hot nights. Hearing the night bugs come up makes my heart pitter-patter. I firmly believe in finding pleasure in the small parts of life. For me, the sound of night bugs waking up for the summer is pure bliss, this is their time to shine. I am a summer gal through and through, it feels like a herald of what is coming. The hotter, the better. The summer heat can arrive as early as she'd like and stay as long as she'd please.

Tea is our signal that the night is winding down. When Greer was a pre-teen, the offer of tea was met with eye-rolling and an "ew, no" face. To her it meant bedtime was not far off. A couple of years later, she'd embraced tea in the evenings. Once the emotions start-ed getting hard and she needed a space to wind down and talk. Our nighttime tea, on the porch or in the kitchen was the time for it. Now she has her tea even when she isn't with me. We've spent many hours face-timing with tea in the flicker of citronella candles. As my energy has decreased, some nights are earlier than others, but it is always how I close it out. So far she hasn't asked why the time varies so wildly. Having tea on the porch with my niece and dogs may seem mundane. But when you have a piece of your life missing, it is such a blessing to have it back. I finally am feeling the exhaustion of the day fully. Ready to turn in, tomorrow will be just as busy. We're having brunch at Erin's café.

Chapter Four

♥

-Greer-

Hard to believe I've been home for a month. In a surprise turn, my few items on the moving truck were delayed and took weeks to arrive. One of my faults is that I am a committed overpacker. Staying two nights? Better pack a week of undies and five outfits. The past few weeks has been one of the only times that has actually benefited me. Putting it in my win column.

Learning how to adjust my workdays has also taken some time. My hours aren't necessarily set, and I am trying to navigate the balance of meetings, workload, and enjoying being home. Having to remind myself that in the office, I would have non-productive spans of time and chat with colleagues. I don't have to be tied to my computer all day with no breaks. Is it refreshing? Stressful? The best I can tell you– I don't know yet.

New habits are being formed and that's what has been refreshing. On my first night, Kayla, Lauren, Surf, and I made a few plans. The four of us had a weekly lunch until Lauren headed out for the Keys. Rather than cancel, we simply adjusted and the three of us go. One of the "new" places in town has been an expansion of Erin's little café. They offer breakfast, brunch, and lunch until mid-afternoon.

It's been such an interesting experience to be home, spending time with old friends. I've truly enjoyed being back and I can't believe it took me this long to get here. One thing I have noticed has started to get to me, is that I'm unsure what my next steps will be. I know I've only been home for a few weeks, well really, it's been a month, but I'm always somebody with a plan and I don't seem to have a plan at this point. A chronic over-planner, I'm trying not to let it stress me out but it's somehow always in the back of my mind. Moving home was a way to decrease that stress and find a sense of peace and I don't want this unsettled feeling to start to rob me of that peace. Hattie and I talked about it earlier this week. She wants me to take time and think about what really matters, where I see myself, and what makes me the happiest. All are very scary things to consider.

Sitting on the porch in the mornings helps. Living in the city, I didn't really have that chance to sit with my thoughts and feelings. There was an undercurrent of pressure, a need to be somewhere, a project with a looming deadline. Having this chance to slow down think about things and experience things it has just been what I needed.

While I have those moments where I feel unsure and I'm not sure what the next steps will be or what five years will hold, I'm trying to embrace that moment. You hear about in the military, they use the phrase "embrace the suck"; well, that's what I'm trying to do. Not saying this part of my life sucks; in all honesty, it's better than it has been in years. What I mean is in those moments when I'm doubting myself, that's when I'm feeling like I'm embracing the suck. I'm sure to somebody in the military or someone who's really gone through something awful, that's not how they would see it, but that's how it feels to me.

That's been another revelation since being home, all the feelings. So, so many feelings. Hattie calls these my big emotions. The ones that take me a while. I remember growing up, Mama and Hattie sitting on the porch for hours and hours. They would talk or, sometimes, just sit and rock in their chairs without saying a word. Erin or Meg would even join them. They'd just be. There's something about being in this space that lets you have and experience those feelings.

In an easier and more fun side of things, reconnecting with my friends has been a blast! Spending time with Kayla, Lauren, and Surf, I feel like I'm young and back in school again. I can't believe that our lives have gone in so many different directions yet are lining back up. Getting to know Hattie's friends has been so nice. I suppose I never realized that Meg and I weren't that far apart in age; to me, she just seemed so much older than me. She was friends with Aunt Hattie and Uncle Davis, and she's had children since I met her. She got married when she was only twenty and moved in next door shortly after she got married. Meg had the twins when she was twenty-three, and they're fifteen now, which means she's only thirty-eight. Which puts us about eight years apart. Time and perspective are funny things.

This evening, we have plans to go to Erin and Cal's house. We're going out on Max's boat on the water. It's been so long since I've spent an evening having a sunset cruise. Max and Cal have been fishing more. Which has been perfect for us, we've had the best seafood so far this season. I'm sure we'll have whatever the catch of the day has been for dinner, grilling is one of Cal's favorite things to do. It seems Max takes after his Daddy in that way too. Hattie is napping so she feels "fresh" before we go out while I finish work.

Next week, Max has a new gallery opening downtown, we're also excited to see the work that he's been doing. He hides away in his studio for hours and won't let anybody see the work until he's happy with it. That's another thing that has been surprising to me, seeing my friend blossom into this amazing artist with this fantastic talent. I am so proud of the work that he does. We are all beyond thrilled that he has another show opening! No idea how he fits it all in. Captaining a fishing charter, helping with the construction company, and working on his paintings.

One thing that has been fun is getting back to my roots and feeling like I am, who I am again. When I lived in the city, I had this feeling that I needed to be a specific person, like I had to be this cool city dweller. That I had changed my clothes, the way I did my hair, and makeup even the way I acted, sometimes the way that I talked. My slower Georgia accent seemed to either enchant or confuse our out-of-state clients.

There was always a need to feel like I was someone else, someone who wasn't true to who I am. Is it age or is it feeling like I know myself better? But I have realized I don't need to be anybody other than myself. Getting back into wearing my bright colors, florals, and prints with sandals every day has been the absolute best feeling! With that I'm off to raid my closet and find the perfect outfit for an evening on the boat.

As we were getting ready for the evening, Hattie has been moving slower than usual. This afternoon she took a 3-hour nap, and I had to wake her up. She was sleeping soundly. I can't recall that happening other than when she's had a flu. I'm not sure if I should be concerned or not, maybe she's coming down with something. Her skin tone is slightly different to me. A lifelong lover of the sun she's always got a glow with slightly flushed cheeks that seem like she's just coming out of the sun. I tried to gently ask if she's OK or if there's anything going on and she brushed me off saying "darlin' I'm fine" in the easy way she has. By the time we leave for dinner, she was feeling back to herself and ready to go for the evening. She said the nap, "set her right".

-Hattie-

We had the most perfect evening last night! Erin, Cal, the kids, and I were all out on the boat. Is there anything like a sunset cruise after a perfectly grilled seafood dinner? Because if there is I can't think of what that could be. It's been so nice watching Greer, and the kids reconnect. Seeing her make friendships with adults that she knew as a child or teenager is special too.

She had a startling revelation the other day she came to me and said, "Hattie did you know that Meg and I are only eight years apart?!?" Of course I knew, but at her young age, it would have felt like a world of difference. By the time Greer was graduating from high school, Meg was raising toddlers. On her summers room from college, she babysat and then when she would come to visit. In her mind Meg was always so much older. I'm hopeful they'll form their own friendship independent of me. Meg is such a gem and has been such a blessing to me and Davis, that I would love to see her and Greer build their own friendship.

Unfortunately, Greer has started to notice that I don't have the stamina that I had before. It's easier to stave off the questions from my friends who aren't with me every day. Erin has the most insights; she and I have always been the closest. How could I not be she's been like my sister since childhood. When Greer first came home, I thought I would have a long time before we had to sit down and have a chat about what the future may hold. But I fear that day may dawn sooner than I had planned.

Yesterday was a rough day, and I couldn't hack it. The last two months have really taken a toll, and I don't know how much longer I can pretend that nothing has changed. For the time being, we'll just carry on and I'll just keep telling Greer everything is fine and I'm just a little bit tired. To this point she hasn't questioned and pushed too hard. She's always been a respectful young woman and never pushes when people ask for a boundary. I'm grateful that she'll give me the time to explain it when I'm ready.

Today is not that day. We have a girl's night! Erin, Sylvie, and Meg are all coming over and Greer has invited the younger girls as well. Ben and Cal have played poker for years together and we've used this as our opportunity to have our own night. A cocktail night on the porch will be perfect. Erin convinced Cal and Max to provide her with some of their fresh catch to get more of that delicious seafood. Since we're on the cusp of summer, we have the most beautiful early veggies that I'll run out and pick tonight. I over planted the beans as usual, and they have gone rampant. It'll be a delicious night filled with food, drinks, and delightful people.

Before the doorbell even gets the chance to ring, I know that our friends have arrived. The dogs head to the door and all sit patiently while whining quietly. Do you know how many years it took to get them all to stop barking? While they sit, I walk down the hall to the door, and I open it to find seven lovely ladies waiting for us out on the porch.

We make our way outside the house is yet again filled with laughter and giggling and a little bit of singing. My favorite things on earth. Lauren has always had the habit of singing while she does small tasks, and I find it adorable. Tonight, she has some made-up little song about the mojitos that she's brought with her. We're going to miss her when she takes her big adventure to the Keys!

Carrying drinks out to the porch, I ask Lauren, "Tell me about your trip?" She begins gushing with details about packing the boat, food, outfits, and how many miles they're going to sail per day. The beauty of youth! One of Lauren's friends' family has a large boat, since they've all grown up on the water, this is not an unusual undertaking for any of them. There's no fear for them or for their parents as they plan a month to sail down to the Florida Keys and then back up again. How different this lifestyle is than those who might live away from the water. When you come from long lines of folks who have spent their lives on the water there's a healthy respect but not abject fear. It's such a blessing that she gets to embrace this part of her life!

Next up, Seraphina starts to share some details of her wedding when Sylvie asks how the plans are going. Seraphina and her fiancé planned to get married here locally in an outdoor ceremony down along the docks. Her love of the water runs deep, having it be a part of the wedding feels true to who she is. All the kids call her "Surf". When she was small, she learned to surf with her daddy, and she could barely be pried from the water. Surf seemed like the natural shortening of Seraphina. Even though those outside of her closest friends and family don't call her that, it just feels like the right nickname.

I know it stresses her parents out, but Surf and Jimmy are planning to move to the Gulf Coast of Florida. With his job, he needs to be on that side of the water. While it's less than a day's drive, it still feels too far for her parents. I can sympathize with the feeling, but I know it's so important to let young ones lead their own lives.

Sylvie shares that she and Ben have decided to take a month off this fall and close the store. She's dreamt of taking a European vacation for most of their marriage, and they finally made plans to do so. That lesson was learned all too well by all of us. Take advantage of plans that you've been making, and don't wait. Sylvie barely contain her excitement as she lays out their itinerary. We are all so happy for her, but also it is tinged with a healthy dose of jealousy. In the best way possible, of course.

Meg drops the bomb of the evening! Her ex-husband called her two days ago and asked if she would consider getting back together. She, of course, laughed her darn head off. That man put her through the wringer and then some. We spent many days and evenings sitting on the porch, chatting through feelings and plans and trying to figure out how she and the kids could make it through. She decided long ago that door had closed. You have to give him credit, though, he does have the guts to call her up. Meg is happy that the kids didn't overhear the conversation. They're always hopeful that their parents will get back together somehow. The twins were so young when their parents split up that they don't remember all that led up to the divorce and the circumstances after. It's better that they don't know that their dad has been back in contact with their mom. We all offer our rousing support for her decision!

Erin and I are mostly observers throughout the evening. We don't have big news to share or bombs to drop, our time is spent enjoying these evenings with friends and loved ones. Life has been so busy and so exhausting lately; it feels luxurious to just spend the evening relaxing. She and I have a trip coming up to Charleston in two weeks. We give the minimum details to the group. Meeting with a new supplier who might be interested in adding different items to the cafe. But that's all we share, for now; there will be time for more later.

Most of the evening passes with laughter and good conversation. The dogs provide comedic relief as they run between everyone trying their best to catch lightning bugs and little snacks that might have dropped. The evenings are getting warmer which means more opportunities to spend time outside and on the porch. My favorite place to be!

–Greer–

Watching Hattie throughout the evening, I am now sure something is up. She has always been the life of the party and the ultimate hostess. I have never once seen that before. More often than not, she re-enters with a fresh pitcher or platter and says, "Catch me up" or "What'd I miss." Now, one of us is likely to be off and running. Hattie deserves the rest, and it seems to be an unspoken arrangement. I'm not sure when it started, and I wonder what else I've missed.

Listening to all of the plans for the summer, it will pass in a flash! Even though we live right by the beach, Hattie and I also have our little escapes planned. Dog friendly, of course. By the way, finding a rental with five dogs is quite a challenge. We persevered and found two- a cottage in the Outer Banks and one in the Florida panhandle. We'll save our trips for later in the summer and can slip away without causing a fuss.

I am already dreaming of quiet walks on the beach with the crazy pups and Hattie. We love to grab pastries and coffee from a fantastic bakery in Hatteras. I can taste it just thinking about it. Since I've lost track of the conversation, daydreaming about our trip, I'll grab the next pitcher of cocktails and a tray of snacks. We had a mix of smoked fish dip with toasted bread, ceviche with tortilla chips, and oysters for "snacks" tonight. Dinner was a grilled fresh catch of the day courtesy of Cal and Max.

In the kitchen, I quickly grab a chilled white and a sweet red (not my fave, but we cater to all here) wine, mix a pitcher of mojitos, and some fresh ice for the little bucket on the table. Task one is complete; it is carried out to the table and met with murmured "yay" and "thank you" messages mingled into the conversation.

Back into the kitchen I go for some snack refills. Lauren joins me to chat while I grab things. We're discussing sunscreens, which brands burn our eyes less, and which just don't work. Laughing over how we've learned these lessons. When a horrendous crash and the sound of glass shattering echoes in from the porch. In a moment of sheer panic, I drop the wooden tray I had been holding; the food clatters to the counter and floor, adding to the chaos. We can't distinguish the shouting voices from the cacophony of barking dogs. Lauren and I run for the porch.

Chapter Five

♥

Hattie is tipped over in her chair, with broken dishes and glass surrounding her on the floor. She's bleeding from the back of her head, and Erin is applying pressure with napkins while talking to Hattie. Her eyes are closed. She's breathing, but it is shallow and ragged. Her arms and legs are twitching lightly. Sylvie and Meg are wrangling the dogs. Surf is scrambling for her phone despite being white as a sheet. Kayla is handing Erin fresh napkins, one after another, and fanning Hattie, trying to rouse her. It is chaotic but under Erin's control. I suddenly feel burning hot and ice cold in the exact second, "Hattie!" I shriek as Lauren helps me sit in a chair. She will not let me stand. It irritates me, but I also realize I am likely no help.

Surf has connected with the 911 operator and is giving our address. Hattie has begun to make some noises. She isn't making sense, but the noise feels better than the dreadful silence. Her head is still bleeding, and she is sweating profusely. I can only think of getting the glass away from her and the dogs. I spring to my feet despite Lauren's protests. She's hot on my heels as I sprint for the door. I'm sure she thinks I'm losing it, and it is true, I am.

I grab the broom, dustpan, and a trash bag from the closet in the kitchen. Understanding dawns on Lauren's face, "right!" she says as we head for the porch. The dogs have been ushered off the porch and are frantically barking. I ask Meg to call the kids to watch the dogs. She's already called, and the kids will get the dogs after the ambulance comes. She doesn't want them to see Hattie right now, which absolutely makes sense. This is hard enough for us, let alone a 15-year-old.

Lauren and I pick up the big pieces and then sweep the smaller ones. All I can think is, "Make a path to Hattie." I don't want her or the ambulance crew to be hurt. My brain knows she's already hurt, but I can't focus on that at this moment—one at a time, Greer, one at a time. As I clean, I am keeping an intent eye on Hattie. Her color has improved; she's making more sounds and is making a little sense. The bleeding is not slowing, which does not help my anxiety about the situation. Why is she not better by now? Should we get her up? I have a million thoughts flying through my brain. The primary one is that she cannot leave me. She is all I have left. Everyone else has left me.

The sirens sound in the distance and it's getting closer and closer. Seth and Sarah are on the porch next door. Meg gives "Wait there" and "It'll be ok" gestures, and both teens respond by blowing kisses in a show of support.

Having wrapped up my cleaning, I sit next to Hattie on the ground and realize I'm shaking like a leaf. Sylvie wraps her arms around me and leans her head into mine. Our tears are mingled together. While my brain can't process the words she's whispering, it is tremendously comforting.

Hattie has gone quiet, but she's moving around a bit and seems more alert. She's squeezed my hand a couple of times. Erin has not stopped talking to her since she fell. Occasionally, Hattie nods very slightly. She keeps her hands pressed tightly to Hattie's scalp. Erin's face is rigid with determination and fear. Almost as if she will stop the bleeding and fix it through sheer force of will. If there's someone here that can do that, it's Erin.

Suddenly, the porch is filled with burly men and equipment. We all feel better knowing that Hattie is in their hands. Questions are asked and answered. Erin and I ride in the ambulance with Hattie. Erin fills out paperwork for the paramedics. She is the most familiar with Hattie's medical history since she goes to all the appointments. This only now strikes me as odd. Why don't I know any of it? This is not the time for that.

In a blitz of light and sound, off we go. Ben and Cal roar into the driveway as the ambulance doors slam. Everyone else loads up into the cars with them. Eddie has had to stay home with a sleeping Annie, but Kayla updates him on the phone. There is only one small community hospital nearby, and we arrive a few min-utes before the rest. While Hattie is taken back to the trauma room, Erin and I are taken to meet with the triage nurse and one of the physicians.

As they begin the conversation, Erin appears rattled and uncomfortable, which we all are, truthfully. She pauses and asks if I wouldn't mind running out to get her a bottle of water from the vending machine in the hallway. Of course, I am more than happy to. The nurse gives me directions, and I make my way over. While at the machine, I decided to grab a couple of bottles since we weren't sure how long we'd be in the ER.

On my return, a different staff member meets me at the door. He asks if I'd like to wait in the lobby with the family. I explained that I had water for Erin, and we were giving my aunt's medical history to the nurse and doctor. He offers to give her the water and walk me to the lobby, sharing that she's "got it covered from here." Which is a super odd thing to say in my book. Considering it has been a long evening already, I am not inclined to argue. I hand over the water. He knocks on the door—the murmuring voices inside pause. When the door opens, all eyes turn to me. Erin is flushed, and tears are streaming down her face.

"Erin, what is it? What's happened?" I cry out. Assuming she's been given disastrous news just now.

"All is ok, my sweet. We'll chat soon," she tells me as the orderly clicks the door closed. Without further conversation, he extends a "this way, please" gesture, and I follow his lead. My stomach is in knots now. Was there bad news that Erin was afraid to share?

Shouldn't they be telling me? What if Hattie isn't going to recover? Has she died, and they're waiting to tell me?

The walk to the lobby is not far, but it feels like miles between it and the consultation room where I left Erin. On arrival, everyone jumps up to greet me and begins asking me questions all at once. None of which I can answer. I explained to them exactly what happened. Quietly, each sits down. Cal, Meg, Sylvie, and Ben look tense. Lauren, Kayla, and Surf look as clueless as me.

"I do not know what is happening, but one of you four had better fess up," I tell them angrily. My face is flushed, and the knots in my stomach are gone. Now, instead of anxious and scared, I am mad and scared.

"Sweetie," Meg hesitantly says.

"It is not theirs to tell," Erin says in a crisp voice from the doorway. The tone and expression on her face brook no argument. "I told you we'd chat soon. Your aunt wants to sit down and talk with you first. It is hers to share. Hers alone. What I will share for now is that Hattie has had some health issues for the last several months that appear to be worsening. Tonight is an example of what she has been experiencing. I don't want to scare you, but I want to let her share the details with you. Understood?"

Although I do not fully understand and am not happy with the situation, I mumble, "Understood," while wiping a tear from the end of my nose.

"Good. Now, the doctor has agreed that we can go in to see Hattie in small groups. Greer, honey, why don't you go first?"

I nod vigorously, not trusting my voice to answer aloud, and the orderly re-appears to take me back to Hattie's room. We take the same hallway but branch off into the secure patient area. A curtain is whisked back, making a sharp scratching sound, and there is my Hattie. Laying in one of those rickety gurneys in an oversized hospital gown. Is it really that oversized, or has she gotten that frail? Her head is wrapped turban style in bandages, and her eyes have both blackened. An IV pump ticks away at the bedside, and her heart monitor beeps continually, which I assume is good. I would never mention it, but she seems to have aged twenty years in the span of an hour. How do hospitals do that to a person?

"Oh, Hattie!" I wish I had it in me to make a clever joke or find a way to lighten the mood, but I don't. I hurry over to her bedside and sit on the edge of the gurney.

"I am ok, darlin'. Seriously, a little bump to the head is all. There is no internal damage, and I'm all stitched up." She smiles wanly. Her blackened eyes crinkling with the smile. Her outstretched hand pats mine re-assuringly.

"Thank goodness! The way you fell, you didn't wake up right away. It was terrifying. Will you be coming home tonight, or do you think you'll need to stay?" I'm reasonably certain I know the answer. She does not look ready to be sent home any time soon.

"I'm sorry that it was all so terribly dramatic, just lost my balance and tipped over. The doctor does want me to stay the night to keep an eye on me. One of the medications I take can cause bleeding, so it is all entirely precautionary but for my safety."

"As long as it is just a precaution and you're truly okay."

"We'll get there, my dear, one step at a time. But, after tonight, I realized I should share some health things with you. For now, give me a squeeze and send in the next round. I'm getting tired, and they'll want to get me upstairs to my room soon."

I lean in and gently hug her, mindful of the tubes and gauze. Whispering "love you" into her bandaged ear. She has a shine of tears in her eyes when I stand back up. This must have been even scarier for her than it was for us tonight. I wipe her tears away, and she kisses my palm.

"I am so happy to have you home. You've come back at the perfect time." Then swats me on the hip and says, "now scooch" and laughs.

Heading to the lobby, I laugh to myself. Hattie is such a character. Death-defying fall to laughing in one evening. What would I do without her? A question I faced tonight and thankfully did not have to answer. I swing into the lobby and call it "next" like a carny at a festival. Two by two, all make their visits and reconvene. Erin and Cal go last. She seems far more relaxed than when she arrived.

Walking toward the exit, Erin hugs me solidly. After tonight, we both need that bone-crusher hug. I gladly sag into her. She finally releases me and asks if I am ok to go home or if I want to stay with them. Honestly, I don't want to face seeing the porch on my own tonight, so I happily agree to sleep over. Plus, they're my ride anyway. Erin surprisingly seems relieved that I've agreed.

Cal and Ben have the cars lined up in the carport. We say goodbyes and part ways. Sylvie and Ben run Meg home. The rest of us pile in together. It is nearly

2 a.m., and we're all exhausted. Hardly anyone speaks on the ride to the house. Even though I am weary to the core, something tells me this will be a night I don't sleep well.

Predictably, I wake up at 6 o'clock. It took me a minute to remember where I was. What's it been ten years since I last slept over here? I sneak downstairs for some water, assuming no one else would be awake. Foolish gal that I am. This is a construction and fishing charter household. Max was pouring coffee in a mug in the kitchen. He broke into a huge smile when he saw me.

"Morning, sleepy head," then laughs when I looked confused. "Want some coffee?"

"Please....." I said and trailed off realizing I heard voices and barking. The entire family, including baby Annie and six dogs, were sitting out on the porch. All the adults had coffee and there was a mound of bagels on the table with tubs of cream cheese. A waft of bacon hit my nose from the grill.

"What in the world?" I say, turning to Max, eyes wide.

"We get up early in our house. Between the café, the job sites, and the boat, someone always has to be somewhere early. It has become a family habit. No matter what time we go to bed. I've got your coffee; come on out and grab a seat." he holds the screen door open for me.

I wish in my haste to come downstairs I'd fully dressed or at least brushed my teeth. At this point, did it matter? PJs were good enough for porch sittin at home and would be here, too.

Max sits our coffees down on the glass-topped table and grabs two plates. The family cheers like I've risen from the dead.

"Y'all are dweebs" I giggle and raise my coffee in a salute.

A massive dog head appears from nowhere and head butted me to add to the welcome. Beefcake is a 140-pound mastiff mix found on a job site that Surf took in. He just wants kisses and has never learned to be gentle. But how could you be mad? He gets his kisses and runs off to join his buddies. His nick-name is "Baby" because he's so sweet. Teensy hops on my lap. The opposite of Beefcake, she is a Chiweenie princess through and through. She spends all day rid-ing around in Cal's truck going from job to job. The other dogs languish quietly on the periphery of the deck hoping for snacks.

My plate reappears with a toasted bagel loaded with cream cheese and hot, crispy bacon. Mouthwateringly delicious. I clap my hands together from delight and squeal "thank you" up to Max who stands above me. He grins and sits next to me with an identical plate.

As we eat, the family goes over the day's schedule. Erin is planning to head to the house and hospital with me. Surf and Lauren are running the café and answering calls for charters as needed. Kayla is front office at the construction company and following up on invoices. She also has to run Annie to the doctor in the afternoon and will need coverage by 3 p.m., Surf offers to provide since the café would be slow. Eddie has two jobs in progress that he has to follow up on; one is almost finished, and one is just beginning. Cal has two estimates to give. Then he and Eddie have interviews to do for two new electrical contractors and a plumber. Max has a charter to take out at 8:30, then a mid-afternoon group. Lord Almighty, this group was busy! My mouth must have been hanging open. I felt a finger tap it up, and Max laughs out loud.

"Breakfast is a daily project planning meeting," Erin explains.

"Without it, I would have no idea where to be," Lauren chimes in and heads nod all around table.

"Like you do anyway," Eddie says, laughing and Lauren chucks a sliver of bagel at him. The dogs are delighted by the extra bagel bit. Now little bagel pieces all have to be torn off and shared with respective dogs.

While I finish my breakfast, I send a message to my boss that I need to take the day off since my aunt is in the hospital and begin canceling meetings. The whole family helps to clean up empty plates and cups, and then the day officially begins. Since I have the least to do, I take over clean-up duty while everyone else prepares for their day ahead. A fresh pot of coffee is made for to-go cups, and out the door, everyone goes. It's a whirlwind, and then it's Erin, a couple of dogs, and me. We decide to get ready and head to the house first. I'll call Hattie on our way over for an update.

-Hattie-

That was not the best night of sleep I've had. The nurses came in every hour for the first four hours, shined a light in my eyes and asked me the same questions. Thankfully, the timing of that was extended when they realized I wasn't brain damaged from my fall. I could have told them that.

Also, this fall was not unexpected. But I don't think they would necessarily have believed me anyway. Which I guess, is probably the safest bet anyway. Long story short, I will survive. Not looking so great at the moment or anytime in the near future, but will survive this round. Guess I should cancel my photoshoot (insert canned laughter).

I suppose the timing of my conversation with Greer has now been moved up. Can't hide this anymore. I could see the fear in her face last night. She deserves to know. While I may not be dying tomorrow, she needs to know what is happening and what we are facing. Thankfully this visit was not another stroke. The conversation will be easier to have now. She'll be hopefully relieved this isn't a stroke regardless of the other aspects. Honesty will be the best policy, I'll have to share every ugly detail. Including how much and how long I've kept this from her.

As silly as it is, I'm worried to about the stress on the dogs from last night. Well aware that I am anthropo-morphizing, but I can't help but worry about them. For a long while, it was just us. They do notice when our routine is off. Last night was a lot on everyone. While I'm thinking of this, my phone rings. I flip it over to see Greer calling. She's right on time.

–Greer–

The porch resembles a crime scene. Blood stains, tipped over furniture, remnants of broken dishes that we thought we'd cleaned up. Racoons had taken care of the food scraps we'd left on the table overnight. Gross but effective. So glad we remembered to shut the door to the house! For all I know, Meg's kids had the sense to do it. We were all in a different mode and securing the house was not one of the priorities.

Most of the dishes and tableware are a total loss, there were a few to be saved but what wasn't shattered was chipped or cracked. I'll set the remaining pieces aside in a box for Hattie to go through when she feels up to it. Some of it has sentimental value, others not so much. None of the furniture is broken. It is easy to reassemble and put the porch back in order once the tables are cleared and it is swept.

While I set to mopping the porch, Erin starts pre-treating the linens. This was the first time I've ever searched "how to remove blood stains" on the internet. Pretty sure that will stick with me for a while. After a quick scrub, they'll soak in cold water and a little vinegar before presoaking in the washing machine. We'll see what can be salvaged.

An hour later, the porch is back together, and a clean tablecloth is on. The table seems like it could be reset for dinner tonight. I text Meg to bring the pups over if she's free. She's at work but sends the twins over. They come with our dogs plus theirs. We sit and visit for a little while. By now, it is nearly lunch. I offer to order pizza and breadsticks for lunch, the twins jump at the chance. Otherwise, they're having casserole from two nights ago. Based on their lack of excitement, I don't ask for the recipe.

Hattie calls with an update and we all listen in on speaker. The doctor has been in to see her. The bleeding has finally stopped from the stiches. If it stays that way for the rest of the afternoon, Hattie can come home around dinnertime tonight. We all cheer and the dogs happily bark. I ask if the medical team knows why this happened and she says it was a complication of one of her medications, but all seems to be in order now. That doesn't seem like a very good answer to me. I started to say so, Erin reaches over and puts her hand on mine. She shakes her head no. For the time being, I let it go. This seems to fall into the realm of what we'll talk about later. Hattie is interrupted by a nurse coming in, announcing he needs to do a "neuro check" now. We sign off and search that on the internet. These must be what Hattie was talking about when she said they wake her up every few hours.

The pizza arrives and we set to eating. I've forgotten how good Capio's pizza is. We haven't ordered it since I got back and yowza have I missed it. There was a place by my old apartment that I used to say reminded me of this, now realizing it was nowhere close. Totally deluded myself on that. Capio's is way better. Crispy crust, perfect savory-sweet sauce, loads of cheese. Perfection in a slice, we don't waste time devouring it.

Erin heads home after lunch and plans to meet me when Hattie is discharged from the hospital. The kids hang out with me for a little longer while I brainstorm a coming home meal for Hattie. In the end, the three of us take a trip to the market and pick up some essentials. Soup and crusty bread are definitely in order after a hospital stay. We decided on a creamy seafood chowder and bread from the bakery. Sarah asked if I could show her how to make it and Seth didn't act like he'd hate to learn. Having them cook with me made it more fun than shopping and prepping by myself.

A few hours later, we have dinner ready. Meg came over after work to relax with a glass of wine while we wait. Sylvie has called multiple times for updates. At half past five, Hattie called and said we should be good to pick her up. After mountains of paperwork and a barrage of instructions that it will take all of us to remember, it was really seven by the time we left the hospital.

Hattie and I lead the convoy, with vehicles streaming behind us. We joked that it looked like a government protection detail. Once we were safely in the house and Hattie was settled upstairs, everyone left us so she could rest and have supper.

I brought Hattie soup, bread, and tea on a tray to her room. We sat and ate together mostly in silence. There were some new pills that needed to be taken after dinner. While going up and down the stairs without help is out of the question for the next week or so, Hattie felt fine to get up and moved around in her room. She had me organize them in the bathroom. I was startled to see another dozen plus prescription bottles on the counter. Not to mention all the vitamins and supplements. Adding this to the we'll talk about it later conversation.

By nine, Hattie is done in. She and the dogs are tucked away for the night. I send an update to the group chat as I walk to my room. As much as I despise group chats, they do serve a purpose. This is an excellent example. I'm reflecting on the memories of phone trees from my childhood. Who would be assigned to call in the event of an emergency, having to wait and keep lines open. My phone vibrates in my hand, and I look at the screen, it's Max.

Chapter Six

♥

-Greer-

My mornings for the last few weeks have begun the same. But this morning, Hattie caught me off guard. I was on the phone and heard noise in the kitchen. Obviously, we were not being robbed. In the last couple of weeks, I've grown unaccustomed to her being in the kitchen without help in the mornings. I could hear her making coffee and figured she wanted to surprise me. To give her a little extra time, I finished my call and returned to bed for a few minutes thinking of how differently this summer was going than I'd planned.

Hattie and I have never had our chat about her health. It is her conversation to have with me. Out of respect for her, I've refrained from researching her medications on the internet. I did look up symptoms and some hints from conversations. None of it is great, some worse than others. I'm hopeful she will want to talk soon but I don't want to push her. Perhaps sharing some good news with her will take her mind off it?

I get up and start getting ready for the day. Planning what and how I'll start the conversation. How do you bring this up? A hot shower always helps me think but today it doesn't, and I find myself rushing. Trying to hurry through the process instead of processing my thoughts. The heat of the shower feels oppressive instead of comforting. Finishing in a few minutes, I dress quickly. I am feeling antsy to get today started. That coffee is beckoning, and I am ready to get this day started. A final message sent, I take the stairs down to the kitchen, a happy smile plastered on my face.

-Hattie-

It's been nearly two weeks since I was discharged from the hospital. The fog feels like it is lifting finally. I do have to admit, I may not have been completely honest with how I was feeling. My head felt like it had been filled with cotton and I could not get my thoughts in order. No matter how much rest and following the concussion protocols, it just needed a little time. When I woke up this morning, it felt like I'd turned a corner. Walking to the bathroom, I actually felt in full control of my limbs and not slightly drunken. There was no transition period either where I felt myself getting better like I did with the strokes. This was an all of the sudden when I woke up this morning.

Greer will be surprised to find coffee ready this morning. Didn't push it with breakfast, figuring I'd start with coffee on day one and be happy with that. Could have sworn I heard her talking on the phone a little while ago. No idea who she would be talking to at this hour. Very few folks are up and at 'em this early. Likely it is one of the dogs.

I hear her footfalls on the stairs and a tentative, "Hattie?" as she enters the kitchen wide-eyed and smiling broadly. She seems wide awake already. We make polite early morning chit chat and Greer asks if I'm up for sitting on the porch. Upon determining that I am, we grab coffees and head to the porch. Greer carries mine. I use my cane as a precaution. Which I still feel makes me look old, but I'll do what I need to at this stage.

Today is the day. It is a Saturday and Greer is off work. She seems unusually tense but has a smile that keeps popping up on her face. It's odd to say the least. She has already showered and dressed. I wonder why she is so keyed up this morning, maybe she's somehow feeling the stress? We don't have any plans this weekend that I can remember. We have all weekend to process it. There will be a lot of emotions, or at least I anticipate there will be. The only question is, before breakfast or after? We'll sip our coffees and then see how it goes.

The day is already warm, the air smells salty and humid. It rained overnight. I pause in the doorway while Greer uncovers the furniture. The dogs play in the water spray coming off each, which makes us both laugh. A couple of them get the zoomies and tear around the yard at high speed. We settle in, watching the dogs and enjoying our coffee. I hate to spoil the lovely start to the day. Greer shifts in her seat and clears her throat. She's smiling but seems a little more nervous now. The smile has gone from slightly dopey to tight.

"Hey Hattie, can I tell you something?"

–Greer–

Now that I've opened the conversation, how the heck do I proceed? We agreed that I'd be the one to tell her, but I wish I wasn't alone. Sheesh, I wish I wasn't. We should have done this together. My thoughts suddenly scatter like leaves caught in a vortex. Hattie is looking at me expectantly and I likely look like a deer in headlights at this moment. If I don't start talking soon, she's going to think this is bad news instead of good news. At least, we think it's good news. It is right?

"Honey, are you ok? Whatever it is, you can tell me," Hattie now appears very concerned. A frown on her face and her brow is deeply furrowed. She leans toward me.

"Oh God, I'm sorry. You probably think its something awful and it isn't. I'm just bungling the delivery because I don't know how to begin."

"Start from the beginning," Hattie offers reassuringly. She's helped me through tough conversations before.

"Okay. I guess that works," I respond and blow my breath out through pursed lips. Yet again wasting more time.

"We've got plenty of time. It's the weekend, and I have my own long story to tell you," Hattie says comfortingly.

"It starts the night you got home from the hospital, at least I think," I begin. Hattie nods slowly, completely unsure where this will go. "When you got home, and I'd gotten you settled. I sent a message to everyone letting them know you were okay and tucked in for the night. After I sent it, like seconds after, Max called me. He wanted to see how I was. You know I am not good at talking with people. But, with him, it wasn't hard. Felt like when we were young. We talked for hours. He called me the next morning and then that night. And he has every day since. We've gone to dinner once and out on the boat once over the last two weeks. He was who you heard me talking to this morning. Basically, Max and I have started dating and we are really, really happy."

I'd been picking at my tank top while talking because I am uncomfortable. When I stopped talking and finally looked up, Hattie was smiling and crying. Not the reaction I'd planned for. She says, "I am so happy!", seeing the look on my face. I finally laugh with relief.

"Whew!! We thought you'd be happy. He is telling his parents this morning at breakfast. Decided to divide and conquer. We all spend so much time together there's no way to keep this under wraps and there is no point to it either. It doesn't feel like a passing thing to either of us. We have both experience those relationships before and aren't interested in a fling or hurting our families."

"Erin and I have talked about this happening since you two were teenagers. We saw some glimmer between you two. There was never anything that we could put our finger on but maybe it was hope more than anything tangible. Not to put pressure but it feels so right."

"That's how we're both feeling. We also understand this is a very new relationship formed during a stressful time, but we've built a friendship over a lifetime. We aren't strangers, we're friends first. Time will tell where it goes, but for now, we couldn't be happier and are ready to move forward with wherever it takes us."

"I am delighted for you my sweet and you have my full support. Here for you always and forever." We clasp hands and rock in our chairs. A warm breeze ruffles our hair and blows through the trees. Hattie's phone begins ringing in the kitchen. We both say "Erin" at the same time then dissolve into giggles. I offer to get her phone and make breakfast for us. I take her phone to her.

On my way back through, I grab my phone from the counter and text Max, "*done*" with three pink heart emojis. He immediately loves my message and says "done" and sends heart eye emojis followed by *"my mom cried...in a good way."* My heart about bursts. For now, I need to get Hattie some breakfast, today is the day we also talk about her health since she brought up that she's ready.

-Hattie-

Erin and I laughed, cried, and started making wedding plans. It feels like a dream come true. Our babies finally found their way to each other! They did it without any push or set-up. We'd always hoped they would end up together. Obviously, we know they've been talking for two weeks and decided today to announce their relationship but to us that is as good as married. The boost of good news we needed!

While I have Erin on the phone, I tell her, today is the day. I'm ready to talk with Greer. She asks if I need her to come over for support. While I appreciate it, I don't think I need it. Feels like we'll be okay. Especially after the last few weeks. There has been enough time to adjust to seeing me "sick". She now sees there is far more to the story.

We hang up and I lean back in my chair to soak up the sun. I am so happy right now. Isn't this what life is really about? Taking time to soak in when you're happy and savoring it. Like when you're eating something delicious. Experience all parts of it. The sun on my face, the warmth in my heart, the breeze on my skin, the sounds around me- dogs, Greer, bugs, all of it adds up to joy. When I have less than happy moments, I pull these out of my bank.

A few minutes later, Greer presents me with a restaurant quality breakfast. Eggs, fluffy buttered biscuit, bacon, fresh fruit, yogurt, and a small side salad to add a touch of savory. A small carafe of coffee comes out to make sure we can top off as we eat. It looks and smells amazing.

Greer sits across from me and smiles. She leans over and pats my hand. She tells me how she feels about being home. That she needed to be here so much and has realized now, I needed it too. I take this as my cue.

"There have been some health challenges over the last year that I should have shared with you and out of a misplaced fear of worrying you, I didn't. On reflection, that was not the best decision for either of us. We can talk about it now or after breakfast." She defers to me. I carry on because there is no time like the present. I've started and don't want to have to begin again.

"After I had COVID, my heart and lungs were not the same. Some of that you knew. But the extent of it, I did not share. Two years ago, I was diagnosed with a rare form of cardiomyopathy. Which means my heart muscle doesn't work as well as it should. I don't get swelling and out of breath the way some heart patients do. Instead, I get tired and have other heart related complications. I also have had a couple of small strokes". Greer is watching me with a concerned but not angry or resentful look on her face and I'm relieved. It boosts my courage, and I continue.

"The first stroke occurred between two of your visits, they originally thought I'd had a seizure. It was similar to what you witnessed a couple of weeks ago. Erin and I were coming home from a lunch when I "fell" from the stroke, she called 911, I went to the ER by ambulance. We held off calling you since it seemed minor. I had no impairments, so I was ok to go home the same day. Erin stayed with me for a few days. The second stroke was about nine months ago. I had some trouble seeing after that for a few weeks and was not allowed to drive. That one was a lot scarier. Do you remember when I went to Charleston with Erin?"

At first, Greer does not answer me but instead is just staring wide-eyed and breathing a little heavily. She seems to need a moment to get her voice in check. Then she says, "I do remember, but I thought you were shopping. You called me to show me stuff you bought."

"We did shop, but we also went to see a specialist in South Carolina. He gave me a second opinion that my vision would return without intervention. I decided not to tell you until I had to. There was not a point to it. I didn't want to burden you or make you feel like you needed to come home to care for me. To be clear, Erin, Cal, Meg, Sylvie, and Ben were all VERY against me keeping it from you. They begged me repeatedly to tell you and to ask you to consider coming home, at least temporarily. I told them I would tell you in my own time," I pause before continuing. My head is spinning as this all pours out. The gates have opened and all of it is coming out now. I feel like I am flooding Greer with the information.

"In the midst of figuring out what would be the right time, visits would be scheduled and canceled. Which was almost a blessing, I was not ready to tell you. Then within a couple of months, you called to tell me you were coming home. My prayers had been answered. I hadn't had to ask you to come home, but you were."

Tears stream from her eyes and down onto the collar of her top. We held hands across the tabletop, both trembling. My own tears fall hotly down my face, I shrug them into my shoulder to avoid letting go of Greer's hand. I need her to understand why I chose to wait before telling her. The hurt is now clearly visible on her face.

"Over the last few months, even since you've returned, my heart has worsened. I'm sure you notice I have days when I am tired and can't keep up. Then the "fall" which was not a fall. It was an actual seizure this time, thankfully not another stroke. The blood thinners prevented another stroke but also prevented the wound from clotting off. The doctor needed to make sure the bleeding would stop before I could leave. Despite having had two strokes, I haven't had a seizure before. Combined with the concussion from hitting my head....."my voice tapers off thinking of that night and the memories flash across Greer's face.

"That is why I was unable to respond for so long when I was on the porch. Now I am taking a new seizure medication. Adding to the collection monthly it seems." My joke about adding to the monthly collection of medications falls flat. This isn't really a time for it but stress does odd things to your brain. I pause again to give Greer time to catch up on what I've shared and wait for questions. The hard ones I know will be coming.

With a shaky breath she asks the question she's been holding onto, "how long do you have left?" Followed by a gasping sob, she collapses her head into her hands. I rush to her side of the table and wrap my arms around her. The same way I did when she was little. Her shoulders shake violently as she cries. I take in a long breath and close my eyes. Why this question? I owe it to her. She whispers, "how long?" into my shoulder.

I can't seem to find my voice. I'm trying to answer. This is why I didn't want to tell her. My beautiful girl that everyone leaves behind. Finally, slowly exhaling, I manage to whisper, "maybe a year or so," my voice trembles when I speak, and I need a few breaths before continuing.

"Unfortunately, combined medication side effects are beginning to make my heart worse. It seems to be worsening faster than the doctor thought it originally would," my voice is tight with tears. I can't continue and rest my head on her shaking shoulder. Greer throws her head back and wails like her heart has just broken. It has. I know that feeling. When her mother was diagnosed and we found out how long she would live, the feeling of your heart being crushed while still in your chest. I wrap my arms tighter around her.

Neither of us move, we stay holding on and crying for a while. As if to match our moods, rain moves in with booming thunder. We have no choice but to go into the house. For a while we sit silently in the kitchen and sip more coffee. Both of us sinking deeply into our thoughts. Then it is time for me to take my meds. I promise this afternoon we will go through them all and I'll explain the purposes and timing.

Greer heads off to take another shower and change after getting wet in the rain. When the shower starts, I hear her sobs. I call Erin. She in turn calls Meg and Sylvie. While I was calling Erin, Greer must have called Max and the girls. By mid-afternoon, reinforcements have arrived. Everyone was all on the same unspoken page. The air was clear, even if it was heavy.

Chapter Seven

♥

-Greer-

Predictably, summer has flown past. Travel plans continued, Hattie and I are in full beach trip preparation mode. We are leaving in three days and there are dozens of items left on the to-do list. It will get done, might be cutting it close though. I'm going to need to call in some reinforcements. Nearly everyone is out of town for the week. Lauren is still off sailing. Surf and Jimmy are in Florida looking at houses. Sylvie and Ben are in Europe. Erin, Cal, and Eddie and busy bees with work. We have Max, Kayla, Meg, and the twins in town. Max is with us nearly every day now anyway, so that has been very helpful. From a practical and emotional standpoint.

Most days are good days and only require an afternoon nap. Hattie calls them her "resets". Might be a 15-minute snooze or three hours of solid napping, either way, she wakes up refreshed and ready to tackle whatever we have happening. Some days she doesn't have the energy to help with more than getting herself up and ready for the day. On those days, it kills me to watch her struggle with simple things. Especially knowing it will only worsen.

Hattie has always been independent, trying to balance helping her and giving her space is challenging. I want to jump in and take over when I see her struggling or see that she could use a hand. What I have learned is that only frustrates her more. Taking care of Mama, we learned that you need to take each day for what it is. Celebrate when you can and give extra support when needed.

The morning of our beach trip dawns with fabulous road trip weather. I wake to the sound of the screen door softly banging shut a few minutes after 5:30. Hattie is talking with the dogs and they're "talking" back to her in their happy woofs and grumbles. The scent of coffee wafts up the stairs. This is going to be a good day, my heart is happy.

Dragging myself out of bed will be a slight challenge. Max and I were up until 1 am packing and prepping. That man can pack a vehicle like no other. He credits years of stacking lumber and tools in work trucks, followed by organizing boat holds. All valuable skills! Bless his soul. We would not be ready this morning without him. Thankfully Hattie kept the old Suburban, "Glenda", she and Davis used for road trips. We were easily able to pack in all we'd need for a week at the beach with room to spare.

I can't resist coffee on the porch any longer. Flinging the covers back, I launch myself out of bed. It's like plunging into cold ocean water, all at once is better. Once my feet are on the floor, the excitement for the day hits. We are headed to the Outer Banks! Makes me feel like shouting. In the quiet darkness of my bedroom, I do a small happy dance as I dress for the day. It has been years since we were last there. Wondering how those beautiful islands will have changed. Each storm along the East Coast reshapes things for us all, but some more than others.

Bouncing down the stairs, I make a beeline for the coffee pot. Hattie has already put a mug and the cream out on the counter. Lately, we've both switched to a splash of cream and no sugar in our coffees, progressing to black as we finish off the pot. Bye–bye to delicious, flavored creamer. All in the name of "health". Honestly, I'll take coffee however I can get it. I pour myself a full cup and head to the porch.

As the door creaks open, the dogs all hustled toward me. Hattie chuckles quietly, "isn't that the best wake up?" I smile in agreement while greeting the dogs one by one. Hattie is settled on the wicker loveseat with her legs tucked under her, I sit in one of the rocking chairs across so we can chat. The air is almost cool enough for long sleeves this time of day. Signals of the end of summer. A twinge of sadness as I think about the passage of time and changing of seasons. Better to focus on today and the excitement of our trip!

"What time should we hit the road?" Hattie asks after a long drink of coffee.

"Checked the GPS last night before bed and it should be just under ten hours with the ferry. If we leave by 6:30, we should make the 2 o'clock ferry I booked." Taking the ferry will give us both time to rest during the ride over from Swan Quarter to Ocracoke. From there, we'll catch another short ferry up to Hatteras and drive up to the cottage. We will arrive after our usual dinnertime, but we'll be ok to eat late. Hattie nods her head enthusiastically while grinning widely.

Her energy this morning is infectious. She is looking forward to this trip as much as I am.

"Once I change, the dogs and I are ready to load up," Hattie responds. She's watching the dogs chase one another through the yard, or at least trying to since it is still mostly dark out. We catch their shadows as they zoom past in the dim early morning light.

We finish the last of our coffees and head in to get ready. Within thirty minutes, we are in the car with fresh coffee and all five dogs. Glenda is fully loaded with a week of beach supplies, food, and the dogs with room to spare. Neither of our daily vehicles could make this happen. Heaving a happy sigh I click my belt and crank Glenda to life.

Hattie is working on getting the GPS and music started while I make sure everyone is situated. Seth taught her how to make playlists on her phone recently. She built us a 70's soft rock playlist, it's our shared favorite genre. Obviously, heavy on Fleetwood Mac and the Eagles. She proudly runs through some of the songs and gets it started without my help. In a surprise to both of us, we are on the road earlier than planned. We are always on time but rarely ever early. Outer Banks here we come!!

–Hattie–

Living by the beach, makes vacationing by the beach no less enjoyable for me. It doesn't get old. Greer picked us the sweetest little cottage with a wraparound porch. We arrived last night around half past six. Even though we had been away from home all day, time flew and neither of us felt overly tired. In all fairness, I did none of the driving. Instead, I was the chief navigator and DJ. A new role for me and one that I am happy to embrace!

Taking the route with two ferries gave us a nice break as well. Being on the water is so soothing. We unpacked what we needed for the night and this morning, got the pups situated, and drove off to find dinner.

Fresh seafood after a long day on the road is the best. Tasting the house specialties is one of our favorite things. We shared a shrimp salad to start and then each got the night's special- flounder for me and crab cakes for Greer. She can never pass up crab. We left dinner full, happy, and exhausted.

When I woke up this morning, Greer had the coffee brewed and was on the porch rocking away. Before going out onto the porch, I take a moment to watch her. Since she's been home, she's changed. In a good way.

While Greer has always been petite and fine boned, she was painfully thin when she arrived home. She's put on weight and looks more like herself. Her skin is glowing, her hair has a glint in it from spending time in the sun.

At the moment, the breeze is blowing and lifting her thick sandy hair away from her face. She looks so peaceful with the early morning sun on her face. I almost don't want to disturb her. Just as I'm thinking I won't, she says, "do you plan to join me?" then turns to face me with a mischievous smirk on her face. I am not nearly as sneaky as I thought. "The dogs gave you away", she says, like she's reading my mind. I poke my head out the door to see the dogs in various spots around the porch, all staring directly at me. Dev is in the chair with Greer and peeks at me from under her elbow. His tail knocks loudly on the arm of the chair. Once they see I notice them, the others make their way to me.

Greer tells me they held off on a beach walk until I was awake. Today feels like a tired day, but a walk should be fine, I'll have to be careful how far I walk is all. A cup of coffee is definitely needed first. I join Greer in a matching rocker. We sit and sip while enjoying the stiff ocean breeze.

The house is much closer to the water than we are at home. We enjoy the stronger breeze and smell of the air. In this moment I am so relaxed and grateful to be here. My head is tipped back against the rocking chair, I am soaking in that late summer sun, "Thank you for making this trip happen," I murmur. Eyes closed and voice lazy. I can't even bring myself to make proper eye contact.

"All I did was drive," she responds laughingly. We both know that's not true at all. Before I can say anything along that vein, she continues, "we both needed this trip. I'm so glad we're here. It's been a rocky summer, and this will be a peaceful way to wrap it up." I agree with a mumbled "mm-hmmm" as I rouse with another swig of coffee.

A walk in warm sand with the water splashing on your feet is unmatched. The beach is mostly deserted since it's back to school season. Greer, the dogs, and I walk along watching the shore birds dart in and out of the waves. She carries Dev, his legs gave up a short way into the walk. They were no match for the sand despite his energy.

True to form, Sadie stays right by my side. She is aging, just like me. But, in all fairness, she always has stuck like glue. I tease her that her guardian is showing in these moments. Her comforting size has been reassuring lately. It seems like when I get tired, she knows and will lean in a little closer for me to rest against her. What did we ever do to deserve dogs? The other three are having the time of their lives running, splashing, and barking. Greer thought ahead and brought a couple of tennis balls to help occupy them on the walk.

"How about we sit?" Greer asks as she spreads out a thin blanket. Her ability to read me is uncanny. Yet again, she's planned ahead and knew I would need spots to rest with a place to sit. She mocks herself for her love of planning, but it is a benefit to us all. She needs to go a little easier on herself.

I gently ease to the ground and Sadie rests behind me like a cushion. I am more than happy to snuggle up to her. Her thick tail thumps into the sand, even faster as the other dogs come our way. Soon dog kisses from Ella and Dev are joined by a very wet and sandy Reno and Pete. Greer cackles off to the side and says, "better you than me." She loves the dogs, but not a face full of sandy slobber. When they turn to her, she fends off the kisses with hugs and throws a few tennis balls to distract. The majority of the pack gleefully chase after the balls, bringing them and some extra driftwood back to play with next to us.

Once everyone settles down, we can finish our coffee and collect ourselves. Both of us grow silent and introspective. Greer has a slight smile on her face, and I dearly hope she is picturing her future with Max. Dreaming of their life and what is to come. I see her happily married to her handsome fisherman–painter surrounded by babies and dogs, living by the water. Finally at peace and with a family of her own.

My own thoughts are more tumultuous. I know there are many things to discuss and each day, I realize I lose a little ground. The speed of it is terrifying. I am unprepared for how quickly everything is changing. This isn't something I share with Greer, despite knowing it needs to be said. It should happen on this trip since we have the time, but how and when are the questions. I waited far too long before and it cost us precious time. How do I break her heart again and tell her?

I know we will have less time than the doctors say I will. I can feel it in my soul but don't know how to explain it. A cousin was a nurse in Vietnam, she said when folks know, they know. No test can tell you. The whole situation makes me so angry and scared. Fully understanding that is not healthy and goes against all that I preach to others. Offering myself grace, this is uncharted territory, I forgive myself for the hypocrisy. I've never been dying before.

For now, though, the exhaustion hits like those waves at the shore. I don't know that I can keep my eyes open. Sadie grumbles and curls around my back. Was that a hint? Leaning further back into Sadie's soft warmth, I close my eyes, and Greer drapes her sweater over me. Dev curls himself against my chest and gives a sigh of contentment. That's my cue to rest. Greer and the other three dogs shuffle in around us and we all cozy up for a bit.

I wake a short while later toasty from the sun and ready to tackle the next part of our day. Greer is standing at the shoreline watching three of the dogs play in the shallow water, Sadie is still wrapped around me like a canine couch, Dev is cuddled up and unwilling to move just yet. I reach around and scratch Sadie's oversized head and she grumbles in her happy voice. We slowly rise and walk to join the others.

As I approach, it becomes apparent that Greer has been crying. She swipes the tears away and smiles brightly at me. One of those too bright, too happy smiles. Before I can say anything, she sighs and says, "things are changing faster than I'd planned," and puts her arm around my should pulling me close. My head rests against hers.

Here is the intro I was hoping for, but I find myself unable to say much of anything. Instead, I nod my head slowly and follow her gaze out over the water. So many changes, so little time. In a moment of cowardice, I simply wait for her to continue.

"When I came home, it felt like I needed to be here. There was a pull to come back that was so strong. Being in the city made me feel like I was suffocating and I needed space and to be near home." She pauses and I nod in encouragement. Her voice is shaking, thick with emotion as she carries on, "Moving home had so many emotions, but none of them were doubt. It was 100% the right call always. Only a few months ago, all of this started to make sense. Before that, I thought I simply needed to be here for myself. That it was about me and my healing. While they may be true, it turns out you needed me to be home as much as I did. No idea where I am going with this, other than I am so grateful for how it has all worked out. Obviously, not that you are sick, but that I am here with you."

"Let's not forget about Max," I chime in with a smile, we can't let this get too serious. I won't be able to take it. There are too many hard emotions bubbling below the surface and I cannot let them out in this moment.

"Him too. If I hadn't come, who knows if we would have ever had the opportunity to get to know one another like this. That's also part of the changes I didn't expect. Falling in love with Max, who I've known my entire life?!? Was not part of my whiteboard I'd used to plan this move." Greer's high-intensity planning makes us both giggle.

We choose not to focus on the fact that she's mentioned she's in love with Max. Whether she has said it out loud to any of us or not, we all know it. There's no need to be dramatic about it. You can see it in the way they look at one another, the way they take care of one another. It is like watching two people who have loved each other for decades. An old married couple who move with comfort built over many years.

"Since you've cracked the door open, there are a few things I wanted to talk about on this trip. Would you like to talk now or later?" I probe gently. Maybe now is the time after all. I'll let her decide how we proceed, continuing to take the easier path.

"I am already crying and there's no more peaceful place on earth, so why not here. Do you need to sit, or would you like to walk?"

"Walking might be good. I can go a little further. Plus moving will make me less stressed if I am being honest."

"Of course," Greer says and releases her arm from my shoulders. She calls the dogs to her and stays within a hands breadth of me while we start walking.

These subtle changes are the things that both hurt and warm my heart the most. I'm not entirely sure how that's possible but it remains true. Needing help and wanting help are very different things. Being willing to accept help is wholly another.

"It is not a mystery to you, that my bad days are happening more frequently," I begin, and Greer attempts to shoo this away with a hand gesture, "don't discredit it, we all can see it." She relents and continues walking. It's a struggle for her to openly acknowledge my illness and increasing weakness. Not just emotionally, it causes her physical pain.

"When the doctors and I were discussing this before your move, the prognosis was one to two years. At this point, I don't believe it will be the two years. Not saying I believe my death is imminent, but something tells me that if I make it to next summer, it will be surprising." Greer muffles a small sob, I continue while taking her hand, "I don't want this to hold us back from what we've planned for the fall and into the beginning of the year. We have so much fun- trips, weddings, reopening's, gallery shows. I want you to promise that we will find ways to make it happen. Even if I can't experience it fully, I want us to be part of it together." I feel myself growing more desperate than I intended. There's a rising panic in my voice that I try to tamp down but cannot. My eyes no doubt reflect the intensity.

Greer makes eye contact with me, and says in a firm, unwavering voice, "I promise you. We will figure it out."

I begin to cry with the pent-up emotions of the last several months. Wracking sobs overtake me. Greer's strength shows through. She calmly guides me to a dry spot in the sand and spreads out the blanket for me to sit on. I don't think I can go further; I cry until my tears are spent. Greer rubs my back and cries along with me. Our roles reverse from the usual and she becomes my support. The same way she did when we lost Davis. She does not know the strength she possesses and how much we both will draw from this in the coming months. Once my tears dry, we sit quietly and watch the waves crash on the shore.

The dogs sense the fun and play time is over for the day. All curl around us and rest in the warm sun.

After a while, we slowly make our way back to the beach access point and boardwalk. I don't have it in me to get back to the house. Greer and most of the dogs set off to get the car and come back for me. Sadie stands guard while I wait on a bench. There was more to go over with Greer, but I am spent. The conversation will need to wait for another moment. She knows there are more practical matters to discuss, but there are so many other things to share. I'll close my eyes for a bit while we wait for her return, it will only be a few minutes.

–Greer–

On my return, Hattie was slumped over Sadie's back and I nearly panicked. Turns out she was completely exhausted and had fallen asleep within seconds of my leaving. The rest of the afternoon she slept in bed. I worried she wouldn't sleep that night, but she did. A valuable lesson was learned. I cannot expect from Hattie what I used to and what she holds herself to. For the next several days, I took the dogs walking on the beach at sunrise and we were back with pastries to make coffee for Hattie before she woke up.

Our final day of the trip, I woke and walked the dogs. Instead of going to get the pastries, we head straight back to the house. I gently wake Hattie and suggest we go together for pastries and coffee. She loves a good hot fritter with her coffee. We also plan to see the lighthouse this morning. We'll drive over and then take in other sights further down the island.

Plans in place, we head out for the day. The sun is shining, the skies are the legendary Carolina blue with no clouds in sight. Hattie is delighted with the weather. We eat on the patio, savoring every single bite. Our sandals scraping slightly in the remnants of sand left behind by the dozens of visitors who've already come and gone. Gulls cry overhead. The warm breeze ruffles our hair. It could not feel more perfect. These are the memories Hattie wanted to make. She's absolutely right, no matter what the bad days are feeling like, we need to enjoy what we can.

The lighthouse is as magnificent as always. In years past, we would have climbed to the top and looked out over the coast. This year, we ask a friendly ranger to take photo of us at the base. I send it and a few selfies from breakfast off in the group chat. We linger on a bench outside of the visitor's center for a while then decide to return to the house. Since it is our last day on the island, I want to pack most of the bags up to let us enjoy the evening and still get an early start home.

Hattie naps with her window down on the way back to the house. She seems particularly tired and pale today, I wonder if it is cumulative and add this to my ongoing list of questions for her doctor. She has an appointment in two weeks. I know that I have agreed to any and all adventures but now I doubt the wisdom of that. Will it take too much of a toll of her?

"Quit staring at me and watch the road," Hattie says and smiles. Tension still clear on her face despite the smile.

"Busted! I can't help it. Wanted to make sure you're ok." I respond.

"Can't an old lady nap?" she quips.

"Well first off, you aren't old. Let's get that out of the way. Next, I worry we've done too much this week. You seem extra tired today. I'm never sure if I should call attention to it, or let it go."

"I am extra tired today and I suppose whether you call attention to it or not, it won't change the facts of it. Can't seem to get fully awake today. It is a little unusual."

"Should I call your doctor?" I'm starting to grow concerned and am certain it sounds in my voice.

"Beat you to it. I sent the office a message this morn-ing, so bases are covered. Wondering if all the sun, wind, and fun might have caught up with me after all." Hattie laments. The disappointment is clear. She likely is having the same thoughts I am.

"Sounds like you've done what you can for now, would you like to nap this afternoon, or we could sit on the porch and read for a while?" I offer.

"Porch and reading seem perfect to me. I think I've made a permanent dent in that bed from all the laying around I've done." Hattie chuckles at her own joke.

When we arrive home, I help Hattie upstairs and get her situated into her chair of choice. I go in the house for books, tea, cushions, and whatever else feels will make our afternoon more comfortable. It takes about 10 minutes to pull it all together. I bust out onto the porch to find Hattie asleep. Despite looking relatively comfortable, I still tuck a couple of cushions around her and place a light cover on her lap. She mumbles a thank you. The dogs circle into their own favorite spots. I settle into read and text Max updates on the day.

Time passes quickly and I realize we are now past lunch time; Hattie still hasn't stirred. I check her briefly and decide to make a light lunch. Fresh tuna salad and crackers sounds amazing. It tastes even better than anticipated. Which is one of the better parts of life- food should always taste better than what you're expecting.

I clean up from lunch and return to the porch. Hattie is still sleeping. She's breathing normally and her skin is nice and warm. Should I be concerned? She has napped longer than this before during her tired days. I decide I am being a mother hen and I let her rest for now while I get to packing.

After laundry has been started, most of the kitchen, and the beach towels have been packed, I return to check on Hattie. She is still sleeping. I try to wake her and can't. My gentle prodding progresses to shouting and shaking.

"Hattie! Hattie! Can you hear me? Wake up. I need you to wake up!" I shout over and over. My voice is at full volume. She doesn't react at all.

The dogs are barking loudly and jumping onto her lap. She's breathing and has a pulse but won't wake up no matter what I do. Shouting, rubbing her arms, shaking her shoulders, no response. Now I begin to panic. I call Erin, she doesn't answer. I curse loudly. My next thought is 911. I know there's a hospital, but it isn't close. Will they know what to do?

"911, what's your emergency?" a distant voice answers the call.

"My aunt won't wake up, she's breathing and has a pulse," I hear my cracking voice, but it doesn't sound like me.

Chapter Eight

♥

-Greer-

Waking up this morning is tough, my face and eyes are tight and swollen, my neck is stiff. There's an unfamiliar scent in the air as I place where I am. The reality sinks in. ICU waiting room. Max wraps his arm around my shoulders and smiles tightly.

"Morning sleeping beauty" and pecks my cheek. I feel horrendous. How does he look refreshed? He offers to grab coffees, to which I hastily agree, hospital coffee is better than no coffee.

While gathering our morning supplies from my bag, I notice Erin is already gone and assume she's at the desk for an update. Visiting hours won't start until

8am but the nurses may have let her in earlier to check on Hattie.

Since Max and Erin are both away, I pop to the waiting room bathroom to freshen up. To my horror, I look even worse than I feel. Although, I have no idea how I should look in this situation. It's been a rough thirty-six hours. Hattie was taken by ambulance to Nags Head, where it was determined she'd had a heart attack at some point during her nap and was flown on to Charleston to be closer to her medical team. Erin, Cal, Max, and Surf got here as fast as they could. Cal and Surf took the dogs home. Erin and Max stayed with me, they've been life savers. I was incapable of co-hesive thoughts. Once EMS arrived, my brain seemed to shut down. I don't even remember calling anyone.

Hattie turned a corner shortly after we arrived in Charleston. She's been awake, talking, and irritated to be here. Which delights us all, including the nurs-es. There is talk that today she may be released to a step-down floor and then sent home in another day or so. This was a big scare for all of us. While we knew her health was changing, we were shocked by a sudden and severe heart attack.

The guilt from feeling like I pushed her into a heart attack, hits in waves. In our first conversation when she woke up, she said, "you had nothing to do with this." Then admitted to having felt off and experiencing slight chest pressure since the evening before. She'd brushed it off, attributing it to the fatigue and extra activity from the trip. In hindsight, we agree that it was a sign of the heart attack progressing. But that's the magic of hindsight. You can pretend you'd have acted differently. The medical team weighs in that the heart attack had likely been progressing overnight and then hit with force that afternoon, walking didn't cause it. Her heart has weakened significantly from the studies three months ago.

Erin is waiting for me when I emerge, semi-ready for the day. She has a smile on her face. "Good news!" she says brightly. I rush over to sit with her. Max enters the waiting room just then with three steaming coffees that smell relatively strong. They taste mildly okay which is an upgrade. Today is looking up!

"Hattie's doctor rounded a few moments ago and will move her to the step-down unit once day shift gets started!"

Max pumps a fist in the air and I reach over to squeeze Erin. Even though we'd hoped for it, having it confirmed is a fantastic way to start the day out.

"Even better, the doctor has been so pleased with her progress that she is willing to discharge Hattie home in twenty-four hours if she continues to do well. There will be strict guidelines, but she will get to be home." A group hug draws smiles from passing visitors. Any happiness in the ICU is shared by all, whether they're involved or not. One of the family groups claps for us when they hear our good news.

The next day passes quickly, and Hattie does so well! We are discharged with a flurry of instructions, a litany of appointments, and a home health company waiting for us. Despite the flood of information, we are home and settled in no time. We do better with understanding the instructions than the last round. She has a few new "friends" as she refers to them. Medications, oxygen available if needed, and a sturdier cane for when she's fatigued. Hattie is tucked into bed with Sadie and Pete standing guard.

While I watch the dogs run in the yard, I have tea on the porch. A cool breeze blows and ruffles through the saw palmettos and mimosa trees at the back of the yard. Autumn is in the air. The rustling in the trees, playing dogs, birds in the distance. A perfect little lullaby. Closing my eyes for a few minutes seems like it might be in order. As I rest my head back, a voice calls out from the other side of the fence.

"Greer? Are you on the porch?" Meg half shouts through cupped hands, trying to project without being too loud.

"I'm here, come on in. The dogs are out with me, but they're playing."

Meg unlatches the gate and comes up onto the deck. She drops into a chair beside me. As she sits, I hear clinking. Then she holds up two stemless wine glasses and a cold bottle of white wine. I nod appreciatively.

"It just felt like this kind of day," she says as she twists off the top and begins pouring, "I also ordered pizza."

"You are a blessing. Hattie doesn't feel up to eating and I am so exhausted, in so many ways. I can't even think what to do next."

"While I haven't been in these shoes, I understand the sentiment. It's like a paralysis. Too many things happening, too soon. Makes me feel like I am caught in quicksand or some sort of mud pit."

"Accurate sister!" as we clink our glasses together. We then delve into ridiculous thoughts on quicksand versus mud pits and which would be the lesser of two evils. Ultimately deciding on mud pits because it would be better for our skin. The arrival of the pizza distracts us from the conversation further.

After we eat, I give Meg an in depth run through of the week's events and plans for the next few weeks. Hattie and I have reached a decision, that it will take our village from this point forward. Full transparency it is. Meg sits in silence for a few moments, swirling her wine in her glass. She utters a few colorful words as tears collect in her eyes. While she has been up to date, she is not used to me openly sharing. This is what has made her so emotional.

"We're in it with you. Whatever it is," Meg reassures me in a tear-choked voice.

"For that, I am immensely grateful," I say with a smile and squeeze her forearm.

"You and Hattie, that's a phrase you both share. Where did it come from?"

"I'm not sure where it came from. I'll have to ask Hattie. But I learned it from her and Davis. She always taught me to be grateful for things. Big or small, it all matters. When we feel gratitude, say so. When it is more than just baseline gratitude, say so. Immense gratitude is the kind that fills your cup. Makes your heart feel full and your whole being feel peace, even if it last for a brief period. Savor it. Hattie's love of gratitude has been a lesson that I've treasured and has benefited me no matter what phase of life I am in. There are so many chances in life to see only what hurt or what was and is being lost. Choosing to find gratitude makes it more endurable. You're able to see the light in the dark."

"That's beautiful. So many talk about looking for gratitude, but living with gratitude is a completely different mindset."

"I agree and think everyone should try it at least once in their life. It may not be for everyone, but it works for us." Meg nods solemnly. She's heard Hattie's thoughts on gratitude many times.

The doorbell rings, and the dogs begin to bark. Meg tells me to stay put and goes to answer it. She returns with Erin, Cal, and the entire family. Hugs and kisses all around. Erin and Meg retreat to the kitchen to put away food. Most of the family joins them to help, which feels very much like a ploy to give Max and me a few minutes alone to catch up.

Max leans to kiss me, then joins me in my chair and sips my wine. We chat through how the remainder of his day went. He rests his head in the crook of my neck while we watch the dogs run through the yard in the fading light. Soon, I realize his breathing has changed, and he's fast asleep. Even though we've spent days together in the hospital's waiting room, and he rode home with us that morning, it seems it has been days since we've seen each other. How can that be? How can you miss someone so much when you've only been apart for a few hours? I suppose that's what loving a person is. The sensation that something is missing when they aren't with you.

In a sound explosion, the rest of the family, Meg, and her twins, rejoin us on the porch. I nudge Max, and he mumbles, "I wasn't sleeping," then shifts to sit up, untangling himself from me. Erin smiles when she sees us, and both of our faces reddened; suddenly, I feel like a teenager busted by my boyfriend's mom. She giggles and says, "Oh, come on, it's adorable." Eddie makes a retching sound in the background, prompting laughter from the siblings. I sigh, "What am I getting myself into?" as I rise to help set up the food.

The remaining pizza is joined by salad, sandwiches, and sides. A full table appears in moments. We join everyone around the table and begin to load up plates. Before eating, I excuse myself to check on Hattie. She's resting peacefully and wakes when I enter. She assures me she's fine, declines the offer of dinner, and tells me to give her love and enjoy the evening. Descending the stairs, I recognize this is another new phase. Hattie will be present in the house but may not be present in events. How can I make sure she is included but not overwhelmed?

On my way past the front door, I glimpse a familiar car pulling in. Before they can get to the door, I swing it wide open. Sylvie and Ben are here, swamping me with hugs, kisses, and questions. Just like that, our village is complete.

Arm in arm, we walk out onto the deck. Greeted by cheers and a chorus of "welcome home" messages. They take their seats at the table, and everyone begins catching up. We ask about their trip and want details, but Ben brushes that aside. He and Sylvie want to be updated on Hattie. As with Meg, in the spirit of transparency, we share it all. Including the updated prognosis since Hattie's heart attack. With her now significantly weakened heart, the doctors now believe Hattie has six-eight months instead of one-two years.

Tear-stained faces mirror one another all around the table. It is a lot to take in. But, as a family, which is how we see ourselves, we will make those the best months possible for her. However she wants or can be involved, it'll happen.

The next few days are spent catching up on rest. I return to work toward the end of the week and realize, I have no desire to do this anymore. Right now, I cannot sacrifice any emotional space or my time to work. Rather than delay a decision I've made, I arrange to take a leave of absence effective immediately. Who knows what the future will hold? For now, Hattie is my priority. Savings and leave benefits will get me through. When I tell Hattie that I am taking a leave, her small smile, without saying anything, tells me I made the right call. Every day now is a "slow day". That's how Davis used to describe a day off with no specific plans. It was one of the rare days that you could make it into whatever you saw fit.

Two weeks after coming home, Hattie's color has returned to normal. She uses her cane on the stairs and in stores only. She says she is starting to genuinely feel better. We agreed that there is to be no more of this hiding or putting symptoms off. She shares them all; I don't care if it is just a random gas pain or a bad hair day; we talk about it now. The deal I had to strike is that it is a two-way street, if she has to overshare, so do I. Our conversations have become very unique to say it in the politest way possible.

An invitation arrives for the wedding of "James and Seraphina" to be held at the Dockside Club next month. We are thrilled! The wedding was originally scheduled for the Spring. Lately, Jimmy has been getting more pressure from his job to head out to the Gulf. They'd hoped to hold off until after the wedding. Part of me knows that is the reason, but also that they want to make sure Hattie can be included as well. The invitation is a little bittersweet. But it's about how we look at it.

"Grab your laptop so we can pull up the registries," Hattie says excitedly. That's my shopping-obsessed aunt. Any and every chance to shop is a good one. I scurry off for my laptop and charger, knowing we're going to be at this for a while.

Having spent a very productive and expensive afternoon shopping registries, I close my laptop and smile at Hattie.

"I have to go shower and do my hair," I say sheepishly.

"It's a Wednesday, isn't it? What is happening tonight?" she asks, surprised. We don't usually have any plans mid-week.

"Max has a gallery show in town, and I am going as his date." I know I am grinning like a fool, and I cannot help it. While everyone we know recognizes we're a couple, going to his show as the artist's girlfriend has a very big deal feel to it.

"You've got work to do! Get upstairs." Hattie says with mock horror and swats at me.

I hop off the loveseat and rush off the porch. Upstairs, I wander around feeling wound tight like a spring. In our shopping fervor, I'd lost track of the time. It is right at 3 o'clock, Max asked me to be at the gallery at 5:30 p.m. My hair can be unreliable, so it needs plenty of time and I've got no idea what to wear. What do you wear to a gallery show on a regular night? Let alone as the girlfriend of the artist? I should have planned ahead.

"Hattie?!?" I shout down the stairs almost hysterically.

"Yes, love?" she responds.

"Fashion show?" I ask tentatively.

"You bet!" I can hear the smile in her voice. When I was a nervous teen and had somewhere to be, I'd request a fashion show of my potential outfits for feedback. She never had a negative thing to say but always guided me into the one I felt the best in.

An hour later, I am showered, and my hair is dried. Five outfits are flung across my bed. This morning each seemed like a great option and now, I detest every single one of them. I spin to face my closet in a panic. Riffling through items in disgust. Why do I suddenly hate every item of clothing I own? I collapse face-first into my clothes, screaming silently.

"Let's stop to think before you get frantic," Hattie says calmly from the doorway. I had no idea she was witness to my meltdown. I wish I had time to be embarrassed but, in all honesty, she's seen way worse.

We discuss hair and makeup options for each outfit and narrow it down to two. I try both on, with shoes and accessories, of course. It becomes a much easier decision this way. With confidence in the outfit we've chosen, I finish my hair and makeup. Then, I get fully ready for the evening, put everything on, and stand in front of the long mirror to assess my progress.

A fashion icon, I am not, but I have my own style. The dress code is casual. Tonight, I opted for high-waisted dark denim jeans, a simple black tank, a light-washed denim jacket, bold earrings I'd picked up on vacation with Hattie, and stacked sandals. Max loves my hair down, so I've left it in loose, beachy waves. One last check, and I feel ready to go.

Hattie is in the kitchen feeding the dogs and warming up one of the 50-ish casseroles we have in the freezer. Sylvie is planning to spend the evening and Hattie said she could take care of dinner. She gives an "aww" when I come into the kitchen, and I can't help but roll my eyes. I am immediately taken back to being a nervous 16-year-old heading to a school dance.

"Stop it. You look lovely! Very artist girlfriend but also still like you," she scolds me affectionately.

"Thank you. Couldn't have done it without you," I say with sincerity and pat her on the back as I angle around her to the fridge. "Iced coffee?" I offer out of habit, forgetting Hattie now has to restrict her caffeine.

I say "gah, I'm sorry!" at the same time she says, "I'm ok, thanks" graciously. I'll get used to it, but man, it has been one of the tougher adjustments, believe it or not. Our blood is about fifty percent coffee. Feeling somewhat embarrassed, I quickly pour my coffee, say my goodbyes, and make my way to the car.

Checking my bag on the way out. Lately, I've developed an obsession with making sure my cellphone is nearby with the ringer on high volume. There have been a series of nightmares that Hattie has needed me, and I don't have my phone. Confirming everything needed is in the tiny bag chosen for the night, I turn out of the drive and aim the car for downtown. The slightly cool night air coming in the windows soothes my still flushed face.

The gallery is stunning! I'm talking jaw-dropping. The last time I was in this space, it was a pop-up boutique selling cheap tops and shoes. At that time, it had drop down ceilings and faded carpet. Now there are vaulted ceilings, with the walls and ceilings all in brilliant white. The floors are smooth gray concrete. A well-designed space to display large-scale art pieces. Max has nine paintings on display. Each impossibly beautiful and enchanting. The complex layers and textures give an ethereal grace, almost the sense that the paintings are moving. Stories to tell, all woven into something wonderous.

It feels like his soul is on display for the public to see. Mind-boggling how a person can be so vulnerable and willing to share with others. Considering that I struggle with people I care about, can't imagine sharing publicly. Makes me even more proud of Max. My role this evening is support. Despite his excitement, there is an undercurrent of stress. I plan to take my cues from him, join him when he's meeting new folks, be involved in the introductions, and step away during business deals.

When the doors open, there is a trickle of people for the first hour. I get nervous that there won't be enough support. The gallery manager quietly reassures me that this is not unusual and not to worry. Shortly after, more people begin to arrive, including some regulars who follow Max's work.

A couple from Savannah have sent their team over to make a purchase for a new build on St. Simon's Island. There are representatives from Miami and Charleston here to make purchases as well. Max is pulled aside by the gallery owner multiple times throughout the evening. By the end of the show, all but one of the paintings has sold and it is on hold while a buyer waits for confirmation from his client. Turns out, all that nervousness was unwarranted. I am bursting with pride. You can see on Max's face that he's trying to contain his joy until he can celebrate. Following his lead, I mask my excitement.

At the close of the show, we make the short drive to our favorite restaurant, the Anchor. It sits right by the water and is open late. I'd called ahead and asked for a table on the patio. A new hostess, Aubrey, is at the desk and walks us to our table. For years, there has been Crystal or Devon. We chat with Aubrey as we walk to the table and find out she's just moved to town and taken a part time position. Crystal is reducing her hours to return to college this fall to finish her business degree. Gotta love a small town; in a one-minute chat, you can learn a lot. Often, way more than you or others may want to know.

Sitting across the table from Max, I feel a sudden wave of happiness that crests with guilt on the wave behind. I am so blissfully happy when we're together, but know that Hattie won't be here to watch our future unfold. Rather than let that be my focus, I reach over and grab Max's hand in both of mine. He stares straight at me. I melt looking into those chocolatey eyes, they have the tiniest little flecks of gold in them too. I could stare all day. He smiles warmly and rubs his thumb along the back of my hand.

"I am so proud of you!" I say earnestly, "Thank you for letting me be a part of your night."

"There's no one else I would have wanted there with me," he responds, pulling my hands up to kiss them.

He looks away from me out to the water for a moment and then continues, "Tonight was the first time that it hit me that I might be able to do more with my art than just as a hobby. I actually felt like an artist. Seeing people come back to purchase again and have referrals from previous clients attend. This evening felt like a dream come true. Having you with me was the cherry on top."

My eyes are misty listening to him talk and hearing the well-deserved pride in his voice. He puts so much of himself into these pieces that he deserves for others to see the value. Max continues sharing about early exhibits of his paintings, taking small pieces to art fairs and craft shows, and working to develop new techniques. Over the years, he's taught himself what feels the most natural and found a way to capture on canvas what he sees. He shares his frustrations when he can't get it just right, and how sometimes that works out, but mostly, he starts over. These aren't conversations we often get to have, and I am completely invested and absolutely caught off guard when our food arrives.

The delicious aromas break the spell. We both realize we're ferociously hungry. Neither of us will ever pass up seafood. I've gone with a loaded seafood pasta and Max chose crab cakes. We take bites back and forth from each other's plates throughout dinner. Soon we are stuffed and happy. Dinner wraps up and Max suggests a walk along the water.

We leave most of our stuff in the car and walk hand in hand down to the shoreline. In a moment of bliss, we sigh in unison as we take in the slightly cooler salty air. Max suggests we go up the beach away from town where it is darker and less populated. I waggle my eyebrows suggestively which makes him chuckle. We slowly walk along the water, talking about nothing of significance, just enjoying being together.

After a short walk, Max leads me to the dry sand, and we sit to watch the dark water. Someone has constructed a makeshift bench from driftwood that has washed ashore. The sky is clear, and the stars are twinkling. I lean back against Max, as he nuzzles my neck. In this moment, I am so happy and so at peace. I whisper, "I love you".

He says, "you better," and bites at my jawline. This makes me cackle picturing him like some beach vampire. "Seriously though, I love you more than I would have thought I could love anyone," he says and rests his chin on my shoulder.

"I feel the same. Sometimes I think, how can this be possible? But then, it doesn't matter. I love you, and that's all there is. I can't picture my life without us."

"Are you asking me to marry you?" he says with rounded eyes, growing very still.

I sputter, "Well, no...I...just...I spend a lot of time thinking...and I...." My face is hot, and if he could see it, I know it is beet red.

"Because I want to ask you first" and he slides a ring onto my finger. I spin to look directly into his face.

"Greer Daphne Lucas, will you marry me?"

I can't even answer. I grasp his face in my hands, and we fall into the sand laughing and kissing. In between kisses, he asks, "So was that a 'yes'?" and laughs again. This man never had any doubts when he asked.

Chapter Nine

♥

-Hattie-

The day after Max's gallery show, I woke up to a beautiful breakfast laid out on the deck by Greer and Max. They were positively glowing, smiling, and moving around like they were floating. When we sat to eat, they could barely contain themselves and spilled the news immediately.

"We're engaged!!," they shout in unison. We all begin laughing, crying, and making unintelligible celebratory noises. Greer holds her hand up in front of them. Revealing her stunning ring.

"I need the details," I plead and start refilling coffee cups. We'd downed the first like we were parched.

"Don't act like you didn't know this was coming," Greer teases me before launching into an account of the evening. It's an account that has likely been edited for my benefit, but I don't bring that up. She is right. I did know it was coming but had no idea when. Max didn't share that part with me.

Before our Outer Banks vacation, Max had come to ask my permission for Greer's hand in marriage. Can you believe that? It was so precious that I teared up for days afterward any time I thought of it and had to keep making up excuses. I pulled Davis and Annabelle's mother's ring from the safe deposit box at the bank and gave it to him.

Greer holds out her hand to show me the art deco style emerald cut diamond ring. The diamonds and platinum gleam in the early morning light. Ruth Anne would be so pleased to know her granddaughter is now wearing her ring. It has been in the family since the 1930s. The ring fits Greer's finger like it has been custom-sized. Davis always used to say that Greer and his mother resembled each other; they must also have shared a ring size. As she pulls her hand back across the table, both she and Max stare down in awe. Almost as if they can't believe this is real. The joy I feel is immeasurable. To think that a few months ago, I was hoping Greer could find a way to be happy once she'd moved back home. Here she is, a beautiful bride-to-be.

Sitting next to a man who looks at her like she is his world in human form. What more could I ask for?

"We should clean up, and you two should change," Max says, interrupting both of our reveries.

"Change? Where are we going?" I reply.

"Taking this good news on the road. We've got to go tell my folks, and we are hoping you'll come with us. Today feels like a day we should be together. You got top billing," Max answers me, grinning widely.

I nod in agreement. How could I say no to that? He is so excited to share, and they want me to be a part of it. "Give me ten minutes and I'll be ready." I walk away from the table in happy tears and cry the whole time I'm getting ready. Waterproof mascara had better live up to its promises.

The remainder of the day turned into a party at the house. Max's siblings and significant others came. Sylvie and Ben, Meg and the twins. Everyone came to celebrate. A million questions were asked. But no one was all that surprised by the news. We could have seen this from a mile away from the moment Max and Greer announced to us all that they were together, we knew it would end with a marriage. We just weren't sure when.

With Seraphina and Jimmy's wedding less than a month away, planning will wait until after. But something tells me this wedding will be hot on its heels. Max and Greer are low-key, and neither likes to attract much attention. A simple wedding and likely on the beach or maybe even on the boat seems their style. For all I know, it will be at the courthouse with a party to follow.

The best part of the day was that it was filled with nothing but joy. The entire group was focused on the happiness and love of these two beautiful young people. Our next generation is about to embark on the next adventure in their lives. No matter what else is happening, that bliss overshadows it. However long it lasts, we'll gladly take it.

-Greer-

Time is flying by! It is already the day of Seraphina and Jimmy's wedding. The last month has passed in an absolute blur. It feels wrong to call her Surf on her wedding day. No matter how much love it is said with, she needs her real name today. She is already giving up her maiden name and taking on her husband's.

By some unspoken agreement, we all have called her Seraphina all day.

Kayla and Lauren will be her bridesmaids. We all helped her get ready and spent the day together as "sisters." It's funny to think that we've always been friends, and now we're going to be family—a legitimate, legal family. I'll have a huge family with more siblings than I could have dreamt of.

Seraphina is radiant today. Her summer glow is amplified, and she seems to shimmer from the inside out. It sounds like I am overstating but seeing her in her ivory gown with beading, chestnut hair piled up high on her head, and full makeup. She looks like a summer goddess. Such a contrast to Jimmy's dark complexion and hair. They're striking standing next to each other. His sand-colored suit and coral tie are perfectly coordinated.

Kayla and Lauren are wearing pale coral floor-length dresses with ivory floral bouquets. Golden ribbons wrap around the stems and gently blow in the breeze. Max and Eddie's suits mirror Jimmy's. All are strikingly tall and sun-kissed. The entire wedding party is an advertiser's vision for a destination wedding come to life.

We sit in a tent alongside the water. A white carpet lines the center with flowers and twinkle lights flashing in the early evening. It creates a glowing atmosphere in the twilight. They opted for a sunset ceremony. The wedding party stands on either side of an arch that is lit well enough for all to see the bride and groom clearly.

The ceremony is a tearjerker. One of Cal's college roommates officiates the wedding, the vows were written by Jimmy and Seraphina. Each includes sweet comments and promises to one another that offer glimpses into their quieter moments together. Listening gives me more insight into Jimmy than I've had over the last few months. Hattie sits next to me and clasps my hand while dabbing at tears in her eyes. I sometimes forget, she has been at the births of each of Erin's children. She loves them as dearly as she loves me. In a flash, we are to the pronouncement of "Mr. and Mrs. Ballard". The newly married couple heads down the aisle to the thunderous applause and cheers of those assembled.

As the wedding party heads down the aisle, Max splits off from Lauren. She lovingly pushes him my way. He grabs my hand, and we exit the tent together. My cheeks flush pink as the crowd says a collective, "awwww". Lauren collects Hattie and they walk behind us up the aisle, with her parents immediately behind. We gather in a smaller tent off to the side and all give hugs, kisses, and congrats to Surf and Jimmy. Today has been flawless for them and we are filled with that high from a family wedding.

After dinner and cake, I sneak away to run Hattie home. She's had a full day and doesn't feel up to dancing. Her heart is full, but her body is tired. She assures me she is 100% fine and will call if that changes. I returned to the party as the dancing began. The most fun part of any wedding! There aren't many opportunities for dancing in a small coastal town, I'll take whatever I can. Max does not share my love for dancing but is willing to indulge me. As we dance, we start to talk about our own wedding and reception. Which leads to happy giggling that can barely be contained. Now that wedding number one is on the books, we feel free to openly begin planning our own.

The family stays and dances until the early morning hours. Alcohol and food are flowing. Erin and I have noticed Kayla's avoidance of alcohol and oysters. We're wondering if there will be another announcement coming soon. Annie is already over a year old and they've always talked about wanting a houseful of kids. Maybe happening sooner rather than later?

We gather for breakfast at mid-morning to send off Mr. and Mrs. Ballard. They're headed to an all-inclusive resort in Mexico for a week. When they get back, we need to help them pack and prepare for the move to Florida. For this morning, we are all actively focusing on the honeymoon send off. The whole group arrives to eat together and then watch them drive off to the airport.

After breakfast, Max and I decide to take the day and spend it on the water. Brady, Reno, Pete, and Ella will join us on the boat. Those dogs love the water as much as we do. Sadie and Dev prefer to stay on dry land with Hattie. Hopefully, the fishing will be good, and we can bring home dinner. Definite perks to being engaged to a boat captain! Plus, I am becoming increasingly comfortable with tasks on the boat and am able to help Max with more things.

Laying in the sun on the deck of the boat, dogs happily playing with one another, Max has several lines in the water. We chat about wedding plans and what the plans for our post-wedding life will be. Obviously, we aren't going anywhere. We've both moved past that point in our lives. Max dreams of living in a cottage he sees from the water. It needs a lot of work, but I think we could make it happen over time. Lord knows the man has the construction skills for it. The biggest concern, the property has been empty for the last several years and is likely uninhabitable currently. My interest is piqued, and I tell him I want to see it. He is absolutely thrilled; he is surprised I'd consider it. Something tells me this man will be in for many surprises in the coming years. We decide to troll past it on the way in this afternoon. Meg works for the county and can check who the owner is for us. I'll send her a text after we dock.

Thankfully, we both agree on a small wedding. Nothing big or expensive. We run through a few locations and suggestions. Then I say, "the porch." Max nods slowly. He says, "that feels right." We look at one another and know, that's it. Getting married on the porch. It does feel right. Hattie's porch is a place where I've always found such happiness, peace, and security. Having it be where we get married will cement it in our lives. Plus, it will guarantee Hattie can be with us no matter the state of her health. We agree to talk it over with her before moving forward. Our backup is the patio of the Anchor. We've had so many date nights there and it was our dinner spot the night we got engaged.

Bridesmaids and groomsmen are easy. Built right in, when siblings and friends are combined, the selection process is pretty simple. I'll have to ask my father to walk me down the aisle, even though I'd rather it be Hattie.

-Hattie-

Using the day that Greer and Max are on the water to my advantage, I set to work on their wedding present. There are some loose ends that need to be taken care of at the attorney's office and with my finances. Also taking time to grab lunch on the square with Meg and Sylvie. Erin has a full day of catching up on post-wedding tasks. She declined all offers of help. We think she wants to cry alone as she tidies things up, we're giving her the space for it. Everyone is entitled to a day of that.

Over lunch we catch up on life and what has been happening. Meg's ex-husband finally got the message that she would not get back together with him. The kids accidentally overheard a tense conversation between them. Rather than push for their parents to get back together, the kids were firmly against and

encouraged Meg to stand her ground. She was pleasantly surprised, and it helped her set an even firmer
boundary with him. Knowing the twins had her back
gave her extra strength.

Sylvie's oldest son and his wife announced their
fourth pregnancy, and it is twins. Which caused a
massive groan from Meg. She offered to support
Sylvie's daughter-in-law if needed through a twin
pregnancy. Sylvie also mentions they've hired a new
employee at the thrift store. She'd moved to town a
few months ago and had been part-timing at the Anchor. Her name is Aubrey, a former teacher from Iowa.
Sylvie says, "There's some story there; I've got to do
some digging." The table agrees that if there's information to be found, Sylvie will find it, and they cackle
like hens over this.

Book, tea, and dogs in tow, I sit down on the porch.
This has been a big day for me! I got all of my business
done and spent time relaxing with friends, it has been
far too long since I've taken the time to do this. Focusing on the fear of being ill and staying close to home has
taken away these moments. No more. I'm committing
to spending more time with those I love, doing things
we enjoy. Whatever time is left will be what it will

be, but spending it with the people I treasure won't be regretted.

Greer and Max will be out on the water for a while yet. Depending on what they catch, we'll have a fresh seafood dinner. It's Red drum season. Love a good blackened Red drum and a side of alfredo pasta. Despite being full from lunch, my stomach growls at the thought. I take a mental inventory of what we've got in the pantry in the hopes Greer will be up for it.

Chapter Ten

♥

-Greer-

We bought a house! It may not be everyone's cup of tea. A dilapidated waterfront cottage sitting amongst overgrown saw palmettos and sweet grasses. Something about the rough condition and the solid old bones of the house called to both of us. When Max took me to see it, I knew we'd eventually make our home there. We called Meg from the dock and inquired about the property. The next day she had the owner's information and we set up time to talk.

The house has a long history in the area and lots of storm damage. The owners were so overwhelmed by the needs of the property that they were more than willing to discuss selling quickly. The years of damage have compounded and are now more than the elderly siblings can manage. Hattie and Davis have bought and sold properties for decades in the area. With Hattie's guidance and recommendation of an attorney, the process was smooth. Within two weeks, we'd negotiated and were ready to get our paperwork in order for closing.

We know full well it will be a year or more before we can live there full-time, but that does not diminish our excitement in the least! The moment we closed, Max set to work on the house with his Dad and brother. Hattie, Erin, his sisters, and I got to work on wedding planning.

The wedding plans march ahead quickly. When we approached Hattie about the wedding at the house, she was ecstatic. She'd wanted to offer the house and yard but was worried it would be too small. We plan to keep the wedding to mostly family, with a couple of Max's friends, but there will be around 20 guests. All should fit nicely at the house and on the porch.

With the small list, and how simple we are keeping the planning, we don't see the need to delay. We plan for the wedding to happen the second week of December. It is currently early October. This will give time for people to make plans to attend and for my dress to be ready.

I've invited my father and Janine, they've accepted and will arrive two days before. Hattie and I talked through my emotions about his attending. I preferred she walk me down the aisle, and even asked her if they could both walk me. She deferred to tradition and said even though she loved me, it needed to be him for tradition's sake. We'd had so many moments and memories together, he would get to have this one. She and Davis had homecomings, prom, graduations, and all of my other life events. I felt guilty that I didn't agree with her, but I am willing to concede.

Dresses have been ordered from a shop recommended by Seraphina. Originally, I had thought I didn't want anything other than a simple column dress. Instead, I fell in love with an ivory dress with delicate lace details on the bodice, capped sleeves, a plunging neckline, and an open back. The lace continues onto the back of the gown and merges with the satin into a sweeping train. Far more dramatic than I'd intended. When I came out in the dress, Hattie and Erin both gasped. I felt so beautiful in the gown. It felt like it was the right one. I ordered it that day.

The bridesmaid dresses are a soft sage green, Kayla, Surf, and Lauren each pick a style that they prefer. For the gents tuxedos are deep blue, not quite navy. The colors remind us of the winter seas. Ordering what we will wear makes it feel so real! Wedding plans are all moving along smoothly.

A few days later, during family dinner, I pull Kayla inside with me. We were in the midst of discussing wedding plans. We'd gone into the kitchen to grab refills. During our dress selections, she seemed to be more uncertain about style, sizing, fit, and overall selection than I've ever seen here. It confirmed for me what Erin and I have been suspecting.

"Hey Kayla, are you feeling okay?" I ask when we go in. She's barely eaten and looks a little unwell.

"Yeah, my stomach is bothering me some. But it will pass," she responds while not making eye contact. I notice her hand has inadvertently gone to her belly.

"Kayla...."

"Okay...fine. I know you've figured it out. We didn't want to steal anyone's thunder, so we are trying to hold off," she now says with a smile and covers her face with her hands.

I immediately grab her in a hug. "Why would you wait? Also, Erin and I guessed at Surf's wedding." I tell her with a laugh.

"You did?!? Geez! I can't believe neither of you have said anything yet."

"We didn't want to intrude, but I want to make sure you get your moment and don't have to hide it. This is so stinking exciting! Go get Eddie and bring him in here."

"You sure?" she looks nervous and picks her lip. I make one of those, don't make me tell you again faces, and she laughs. "Hey Eddie, can you and Max give us a hand?"

They come in and she tells Eddie that it's time. Eddie has to put his hand over Max's mouth to keep him from shouting and ruining the surprise. Kayla and Eddie step into the living room to confer on how they want to announce it.

I put Max to work helping me refill plates and plat-ters. He leans in, wraps his arms around me, and says, "how long before we get to start making our baby announcements?" I feel warm from the inside out and I know my cheeks are red. How long will it be? We've talked babies but who knows what our future will hold. "Soon my love" is the only answer I give. With a quick smooch, I tell him to get a move on and we take the plates back to the porch to wait for Kayla and Eddie.

As predicted, the family is over the moon! Two weddings, and a new baby. This year was unpredictable but one for the books.

-Hattie-

Greer is out when I start to feel unwell. I know I should call her and let her know but they are working on finalizing some wedding plans tonight with Max's family. I leave the door unlocked, take my phone upstairs with me, and go up to lie down. I saw on a show once that you should leave the door unlocked in case of an emergency, then the fire department won't break it down. I don't feel that bad, but something is off.

Perhaps wearing my oxygen for a little while will help. I lay down and turn the concentrator on. As a precaution, I sent Meg a text to ask if she was home. She sends back that she will be in about fifteen minutes. I ask her if she's up for visiting this evening. She tells me to give her about foty-five minutes and she'll be right over, asking if I need anything. I decline but tell her the door is unlocked and to let herself in when she arrives.

"Hattie! Hattie! Wake up!" I startle awake to Meg shaking my shoulders. My oxygen is still running, and

I must have fallen soundly asleep. The lights were off except for the hallway light.

Meg is still talking, but I am only now realizing what she is saying, "How long have you been in bed? You scared the daylights out of me. I could have come sooner."

"What time is it?" I croak out, the oxygen has made my mouth painfully dry. Meg hands me a glass of water.

"It's after 8 p.m., I'd texted to tell you that I was running a little behind. But I didn't hear back from you. When I came in, the lights were all off, and the dogs were whining and scratching to go out the back door. I found you up here, and you weren't responding. I was seconds away from calling 911."

"There's no need for all that. I am sorry that I scared you. Tonight wasn't my best night. Greer is out and I suspected that I shouldn't be alone. Rather than fess up, I thought I'd try to be subtle and ask if wanted to just come over to visit."

"Are you having pain or shortness of breath? Do you need me to call Greer?"

I shake my head, suddenly embarrassed by the stress I've caused my friend. This isn't like me. I don't spring things on people with no warning. The times when I do ask for help, I'm always clear about what I need. This evening though, I'm not sure what came over me.

"You scared the daylights out of me! I thought you were having another heart attack." Tears are in Meg's eyes with this last part, and I realize how badly I've scared her. We both are quiet for a few minutes. Meg takes a seat on the edge of the bed. Her breath begins to steady. "I am glad you called rather than be alone and need help. Have you eaten?" I shake my head, and she offers to make us dinner.

After we have recovered from the initial shock and stress of the evening, Meg and I have a nice couple of hours sitting on the porch. We shared some left-over lasagna and salad Greer made last night, pairing it with a dry white wine that Sylvie and Ben brought back from Europe. Was a delicious meal with minimal effort, much needed after that start to our evening.

I catch Meg up on the most up-to-date wedding happenings and my plans for the "kid's" gift. She gives me an overview of the twins' latest school projects, newest hobbies, and the recent office drama. All in all, it turned into a pleasant evening.

The front door opens, and Greer sweeps in. She's smiling and happily drops into a chair across from us. She pours herself the remainder of the wine and unwraps a plate of goodies she's brought home from Erin's. Perfect for my sweet tooth- which remains entirely undiminished. A collective groan of delight over the gooey chocolatey goodness of the brownies. There are perks to having a friend who runs a café. All the goodies!

Neither of us shared the earlier part of the evening with Greer. Instead, Meg asks her to tell us about the house and property. Since Meg had been involved in the initial inquiry into the property, she's especially interested in the progress. It will require an overhaul of most of the house. Max and Eddie are beginning the work by clearing the road and driveway of brush and trees that have come down in storms over the last few years. From there, a dock will be repaired to allow faster access to the house.

Greer grows increasingly animated, talking about plans for the interior and exterior and how they'd like the kitchen and bedrooms to be. Restoring the sleeping porch to use for outdoor entertaining and dining. Watching her share the next phases of her life is bittersweet. I am happy to know she will be loved, safe, and well taken care of. In the same moment, it crushes my soul to know I won't see her home finished and filled with babies. Some days I doubt I will make it to her wedding in a few short months. I'll do whatever I need to be there. Whatever ounce of strength I need to pray for, I will. I shake these thoughts away and return to the conversation. She is in the happiest moments of her life, and I want to be right here with her. She deserves it more than anyone I know. It is the best I can do for both of us.

Meg is sharing her thoughts on all the plans and how exciting it is. I catch Greer's eye and smile, so proud of her and Max. She dips her head briefly, and tears shine in her eyes when she looks up. How does she always know? She's always had the uncanny ability to read my heart and mind. While Meg chats on, Greer holds my gaze and smiles back at me. Her chin quivers slightly, and I nod. In unison, we clear our throats and refocus. This unspoken conversation passes for now.

A short while later, Seth calls out from their deck asking if he and Sarah can make brownies. Meg takes that as her cue to head home before chaos ensues in her kitchen. She says her goodbyes and I thank her for making time for me earlier. We watch her walk across our yards and into her back gate. Sarah and Seth come out to say goodnight before continuing their crusade for late night baking and movies.

Greer and I wave, the dogs run in happy circles realizing something is going on but not having a clue what it might be. After they've gone in and the porch light is off, we return to our spots on the porch. Greer grabs the lighter. She walks around lighting each of our candles, wine bottle torches, and bug lights. Once we are fully ensconced in fiery glow, she turns off the porch lights.

We sit quietly, enjoying the flickering light and watching the stars. The dogs curl into their spots with us under blankets and on chairs. A sense of calm and peace falls over us. Greer leans her head back against her rocker and sighs. There's no point in asking, she'll talk if she wants. Besides, I know what she means. We're tired and have a lot of feelings that don't easily have words put to them. It's nice to just sit and soak in the quiet together. These times are few and far between suddenly.

"What will I do when you aren't there?" Greer whispers with her eyes closed.

"You'll do what you've always done. You'll keep going," I tell her. My voice is tight. I do not want to cry.

"I could keep going because you were there..." she trails off, her chest shuddering.

I struggle with what to tell her next. I don't want her to feel pain and don't know how to tell her to take her next steps. While I collect myself, Reno jumps onto her lap and snuggles up to her neck.

"Do you remember when your Mama was dying? And we first talked about it?

"Of course, I was fifteen and it felt like my world would end."

"Did it end?"

"No. It felt like I wouldn't survive though."

"How did you make it through?"

"I had you and Davis with me. You loved me through it. Kept me safe. Made me feel like I still had a home and family."

"And what happened when Davis died? When I felt like I couldn't go on? How did you help me?"

"I stayed with you and made sure you felt safe and loved."

"Did we come out of those ok?"

"Hurt, but ok."

"We did because we had love. I know you've always had me by your side when things have hurt you, and you've felt alone. But now it isn't just me. Now, you have Max and a whole family and a lot of friends besides me to love you. That's how you'll make it. The same way you always have. Hurt but loved. You'll be ok."

"I can't do it," Greer sobs and clings to Reno.

"You can and you must. If I could stay with you forever, I would, and you know that. It absolutely crushes me to think of you having to keep going, hurting without me. I would trade anything to take that away. I never wanted to be the cause of your pain. You've lost so much in your life. This has all been too much. But it is what it is, my love. All we can do is enjoy what we have together now and make the most of it. Which is disgustingly cliché." Her tears briefly turn to a choked laugh at this.

"Every plan Max and I make, there's a tinge of will you or won't you be here to see it. I want you to be here for all of it. Reality strikes that it isn't possible, and that derails my excitement. I know Max senses it but doesn't want to bring it up. We plan like you will be here for all of it. Tonight, Kayla and Eddie announced they're having another baby. Rather than be as happy as I should, all I could think was, will Hattie meet any of my babies?" her tear-stained face is lined with pain as she talks. No doubt mirroring my own. We both know that I likely won't ever meet her children unless she has a child in the next few months.

With this, we once again fall silent. After a few minutes, Greer comes over to sit with me on the loveseat. She rests her head on my shoulder. We sit, and each takes time to think about our conversation.

True to form, instead of continuing, we move on. Greer points to a constellation in the clear night sky and asks me which it is. She knows them as well as I do. To appease her, I tell the story of the three sisters. Greer listens as if it is the first time she's heard it. Enraptured by each detail of the old story, just like when she was a child. The dogs sleep, and we chatter about inconsequential things late into the night. Bringing a bit of balance back into our evening. Both of us start yawning more than talking; we put the candles out and call it a night.

Chapter Eleven

-Greer-

This morning started out clear, bright, and chilly. A classic mid-November day. We are planning to be on the boat for a day of fishing and family time. These days, Hattie's oxygen is a member of the group. We no longer grab a quick bag of snacks, the dogs, and off we go.

Our routines are slightly more complex, but worth it to have her with us. She tries to say she'll be okay if she stays home, but anyone who's met this woman knows. She's never happier than when she's on the water. Watching her sit with her head leaned back, eyes closed, she is at peace. I love to see her hair being whipped around by the salty air. It makes her laugh every single time.

Our best intentions did not quite go as planned. I spilled coffee twice and had to change after completely soaking my jeans on the last round. Then, I locked the keys in the car. After thirty minutes of frenzied searching, Hattie found the spare set in the office drawer.

Sadie and Reno refused to leave the house; they apparently were not up for a day on the water. We texted Meg to see if she'd mind sending one of the twins over later to check on them. Instead, she offered to have them bring the dogs over for a puppy play date. Finally, we made it out the door forty-five minutes late.

On arrival at the dock, Hattie waits on one of the benches while I run over to check in with Max. While she was waiting, Dev and Ella rolled in fish remnants left behind at the cleaning station. Thankfully, Pete had the good sense to be grossed out by it. This led to an impromptu swim while Max situated Hattie and our belongings on the boat. It's not our best start to a day on the water, but it definitely will be memorable. Within a few hours, we'll all be laughing about it.

An hour into our cruise, Hattie leans over and puts her head on my shoulder. I snake my arm around and pat her back. It is much cooler out on the water than I'd guessed it would be. We're bundled up in jackets and hats to our chins, with a blanket over our legs. A pile of dogs are tucked in around us. Some are smellier than others. Hattie begins sharing memories of the weeks leading up to her wedding with Davis.

"Your mama and Erin concocted all these wild plans for parties. They were convinced that we'd never spend time together again once I married Davis."

"Pretty sure they misjudged that one," Max pipes up from the helm.

Hattie chuckles and continues on, "They certainly did! The best was when Erin borrowed a convertible from her uncle and drove us down to St. Augustine for a weekend. The intention was to party and make it memorable. It was memorable, for sure. The looks on Erin and Annabelle's faces have stuck with me after all these years." Hattie's shoulders jiggle as she laughs before she can finish.

"We arrived at the hotel with a few hours of sunlight left, thankfully. It was advertised as a 'vacationer's paradise' with a pool, tennis court, and lounge with live music. Twenty or thirty years before it would have been a paradise. What we arrived at seemed to be more on the verge of being condemned and possibly carrying several contagious illnesses. We took one look, turned on our heels, and went back to the car.

The next several days were spent bouncing from one place to another, sleeping in cheap beachfront hotels and soaking up the sun during the day. It could have been a total disaster, but it ended up being a fun girl's weekend anyway." She continues with stories of the adventures they had throughout the weekend, the people they met, and the mischief they got into. None of which they shared on the return home. As far as their families knew, all went according to plan.

"Is this why you're so obsessed with getting to hotels in the daylight?" I tease. Thinking of them in a disease-riddled, foul hotel with a funky smell and questionable bedding. Picturing one of those TV news specials.

"Some fun is not worth repeating," Hattie looks at me with one eyebrow raised. I always wondered why she made us get to hotels right at check-in time, now it makes much more sense.

Hattie shares more stories of double dates gone awry, dress-fitting snafus, and seating chart family meltdowns. She shares a few from Erin and Cal's wedding, Mama and Joel's. So many funny stories that we've not heard before. Over the course of the afternoon, Max and I felt like we got to know them all better through Hattie's memories. She has always been a storyteller, and it's fun to hear tales from her youth.

Hattie nods off as we glide along the coast. I make sure she is covered and warm, with dogs surrounding her to keep her cozy. Once she is situated, I slip to the helm to spend time with Max. He tucks me into his warm waterproof coat, and I squeeze in between him and the wheel. In a few minutes, I am warmer than I have been all day.

"Is this what it's going to be like having a husband?" I turn my face up to ask.

"Like what?" Max responds, looking a little confused but also happy.

"Safe, warm, and happy," I say, snuggling even deeper into his coat.

"Always," he says and laughingly kisses the top of my buried head. We ride along quietly in warm contentment. Max's chin rests on the top of my head. Despite the appearance of stillness, I can feel the muscles in his chest and arms continually working as he guides the boat through the water.

"Look over to the right," he murmurs after a few minutes.

"Oooooh, is it dolphins?" I struggle to get a good view.

"Even better...it's our home," Max squeezes me tightly when he responds. I sigh and feel that happiness from my toes all the way up to my scalp. It literally tingles when I hear the emphasis on "our" in that sentence. Even though it will be a long time before we truly make our home here, knowing that we are shaping it into our space to raise our family in is a dream come true. A dream I didn't even know that I had.

Seeing the progress surprises me. The brush surrounding the house has been mostly cleared away, and you can see the old, screened porch from the water. Live oaks with Spanish moss slung between branches frame it beautifully. From this distance, the house doesn't seem to be in such bad shape, and if you squint just right, it looks like the photos from long ago.

"Have you been sneaking out here to work?" I question with mock offense.

Max blushes slightly, "Here and there when I have extra time, I stop by."

"Don't be embarrassed! I love that you come out when you can work on the house and I'm a little jealous that I don't get to work here as much. Let me know next time, and I'll come with you."

"You've been busy with the wedding plans and everything else," his voice slowly fades. We both know he means Hattie's failing health has needed more time, but he doesn't want to say it aloud. His grip around my waist tightens slightly, and I lean back against his chest. The waves lap against the side of the boat as we sit and stare at the house. Watching the moss blow in the trees is hypnotic. Breaking the spell, one of the dogs gets up with a loud grumble and stretches. Clearly bored now that we're sitting still. I turn and see Pete bowed low and wagging his tail. He ambles to us and rests his chin on my lap.

"Can we dock and walk them for a minute?" I ask hopefully, knowing Hattie will love to see the house.

"Of course, I worked on the dock a bit, and it's safe enough for now," Max replies and starts the boat engine up slowly. To free him up to maneuver the boat, I untangle myself and go back to wake Hattie. She is as delighted to see the house as I thought she would be.

As Max pulls the boat alongside the dock, I hop out to tie it off. It occurs to me that plenty can be learned in a few short months. Having grown up near the water, I had a moderate knowledge of boats. Dating and now marrying a charter boat captain has really amped up that knowledge and confidence around boats. Not saying I want to drive the boat anytime soon, but I am no longer anxious with sweaty palms when Max asks me to help with small tasks.

We get Hattie and the dogs off the boat and onto the dock. Dev and Ella still carry their fishy perfume, lifting them out was a smelly adventure. Wonder how many baths it will take for them to be back to normal?

The walk up the dock to the house is not long, but it gives us time to take in more of the work that's been done in the past two weeks. We walk slowly with Max carrying Hattie's oxygen tank instead of letting it bump around on the dock.

Max points out to Hattie areas where trees have come down in the last few storms and had fallen over the drive, covering entire sections of the yard. A large burn pile is off to the side of the house in a clearing. Max, Eddie, and Cal have been burning brush as they cut through it. He proudly points out an area back from the house with a sweeping view of the water. He and Hattie play a guessing game of what will be in that spot. After a few tries, she nails it, "a studio?" Max beams at us, he is delighted to have a dedicated space on the property to use as a studio and potentially a showroom further down the road. We plan to get the building put up so it is functional for Max as soon as we swing it.

The house will take far longer to be ready, and I am anxious for him to have this. He talks Hattie through his vision for the studio and the house. Listening to them talk about the house and hearing the enthusiasm in Max's voice makes me smile. His excitement is palpable, and I see that Hattie is as enchanted as I am. Hattie and I link arms and walk beside Max as he guides us around the back of the house. The dogs happily bound ahead of us, thrilled to be running and wrestling after hours on the boat. Their tails wagging in unison adds to the joy we're all feeling in the moment.

We spent about an hour walking around the property and picturing how it would look. By then, the mist was turning to light rain. It was agreed that our day on the water was at an end, and we should go home for dinner. A chilly and damp ride finished our day, and by the end, we were ready for something hot and cozy at the house.

Max lit a fire while I started dinner. At my insistence, Hattie went upstairs for a shower and to rest before we ate. Her eyes had been drooping, and her color was a bit off. Signs indicating today had been too much for her. I'd texted Meg when we were at the dock to let her know we'd be home sooner than planned.

Seth had brought the dogs home and delivered a fresh batch of yeast rolls Sarah and Meg had baked before we arrived. He was walking across the yard when we pulled in the drive. The rolls were still hot, melted butter glistening on the tops. Freshly baked bread must be one of the best smells in the world, at least in my opinion. They will go perfectly with some seafood chowder I made a few weeks ago and popped into the freezer. The soup plunks satisfyingly from the plastic container in the soup pot. It lands with such a firm thud that Max looks up from his spot by the fireplace and laughs. The few dogs in the living room spin their heads in curiosity and hopefulness they'll get some too. Dinner prep always holds their interest.

Fire in progress, soup beginning to thaw. I pour us some wine and walk to the stairs to hear if the shower is still running. It isn't, but I can hear Hattie softly talking to a couple of the dogs upstairs with her. I call up to see if she'd like some wine while she rests, but she doesn't answer. Unconcerned, I return to the kitchen.

Max and I chat through a few remaining wedding plans, mostly discussing the logistics of the day of and day after. Since it will be so small, we won't have a ton to do, but there is always more than you'd think there will be. In addition to the actual preparation and ceremony, the stress of Joel and Janine coming into town and involving them in the festivities. I continue to feel torn; I do want them at the wedding, but I am still unsure how much I want them to be included. Rather than feel like a father and stepmother, they feel like distant relatives that I have to give starring roles in the wedding. Max knows my struggle and supports me. Despite feeling so torn, I've committed by inviting them and asking Joel to walk me down the aisle. I did draw the line and tell Hattie she had to be the one who stands to give me away. Joel may be my birth father, but Hattie helped raise me and was my legal guardian. Hattie and I had a very tense conversation about it. She ultimately caved and landed on my side. She said there is only so much tradition one can stand on that it is a day to celebrate Max and me. We need to make it special and have those we love participate how we choose. Prior to that, I don't think Hattie and I had fought since I was a teenager. Once it was over, I cried for an hour with relief that we could move on.

The soup warmed through, Max offers to dish it up while I checked on Hattie. Since it had been nearly twenty minutes, I assumed she would be sleeping, or at least I hoped she would have closed her eyes for a bit. The lights were all off upstairs, and it was silent. I crept up the staircase and cracked open Hattie's door. She was tucked into bed with three dogs curled around her, including Brady. Experience has taught me that I am not comfortable simply peeking at her. I approached on tiptoes, giving the dogs a "shush" motion with my finger to my lips. Tails thumped and eyebrows raised, but none made a sound.

Hattie's oxygen concentrator hums loudly beside her bed. As I lean in to check on her, she murmurs, "I'm fine, my dear, just tired. I promise. The hot shower after a day on the water did me in. Save me some supper, and I'll try to be down in a bit." I pull her covers up and brush my lips against her forehead. She blows an air kiss without opening her eyes. As I turn to go, she doesn't stir, and the dogs all maintain their spots, tails still softly thumping when I make eye contact. She is safe and sound for now.

Morning dawns and we realize Hattie never came down for her supper. I'd put her dinner aside in the fridge, ready to warm up quickly but this morning it is untouched. I make a pot of coffee and put some pastries in the toaster oven to warm up. Thinking Hattie must be starving after having nothing to eat last night. While the pastries heat up, I go upstairs to check on Hattie and let the dogs out. We'd left her door cracked the previous night so they could come in and out if needed, yet all are still upstairs and quiet.

I get a prickle of anxiety up the back of my neck. Something feels wrong. I knock quickly on Hattie's door. She doesn't respond, I can hear the dogs quiet whining and light scratching. I fling the door open without waiting.

"Max!!!" I scream and run to Hattie's side. She is sprawled over the edge of the bed, arms and legs at odd angles. Her face is gray, and she's wet with sweat.

The dogs are now pacing frantically around us. She's breathing, it is shallow and there's rattling in her chest. It's like something is caught, and she can't cough it up. I try to sit her up to ease her breathing. She's heavier than I thought, I am not strong enough to get her fully upright. Max appears at the doorway and rushes to me. He quickly helps me reposition Hattie. We put her oxygen mask on her face and turned it up.

"Stay with her and talk to her. Try to wake her up. I need my phone to call 911," I instruct and race from the room.

"911, what's your emergency..."It feels like déjà vu as I say, "It's my aunt; I can't wake her up. She's breathing and has a pulse." The operator collects basic information, and I thunder back up the stairs to give her an update.

Max sits in Hattie's bed with her resting back against his chest. He's holding her oxygen and supporting her head. Using the edge of a blanket, he dabs the sweat from her forehead. She isn't responding to much of what he's saying to her, but her eyes are fluttering, at least. Her breathing seems a little better in this position.

I update the operator, and she offers me advice on helping Hattie until the ambulance arrives. While I am collecting medications and what Hattie will need from her room, I start another group text to let everyone know what is happening. Texts arrive in rapid succession despite the early hour.

The sirens blare in the driveway. I run down the stairs as the paramedic pounds on the front door. Once again, we find ourselves surrounded by a flurry of activity and life-saving measures. This time, there is a distinctly different feeling; it makes me anxious and nauseous. There is more urgency and more tension from the team that has arrived.

Max and I are ushered away from the bedside. In a few moments, they've made the decision to place a breathing tube in Hattie. Her oxygen is too low, and they're concerned her already strained heart won't be able to tolerate it. I sob, watching them put the tube in. Max turns me to face him while they work. I can't take watching her poor little body being poked and prodded. With a rush, they finish and make their way down the stairs and out the door. I asked to ride with them, but they advised against it and told us to meet them at St. Agnus.

Max and I rush to get out of the house. Both of our phones are ringing, our family and friends are checking in. They're desperate to know what is happening and to help somehow. Plans are made to care for one another, work, and the dogs in progress. Everyone steps in for one thing or another. My brain feels like it has shuddered to a stop. I can't seem to make sense of things fully. The moment those ambulance doors closed. I went into autopilot mode. I know tears are falling; I can't stop them or deal with them. They run freely down my face and onto the sweatshirt I threw on over my pajamas.

Today is the day. Today is the day I may never see Hattie again. Those doors closing may have been my chance to say goodbye. It circles in my head on a loop. I've lost her. What if that was it?

Chapter Twelve

♥

-Greer-

We screeched to a halt in the Emergency parking lot and rush inside. I hear Max telling the front desk staff who we are and who we are there to see. We're seated in that dreaded room to the side of the waiting room. The one they take you to when things aren't going well. It's quiet and beige, and the lighting is dim. Tissue boxes are strategically placed on flat surfaces. My brain takes inventory of the boxes like it is something I'll need to keep track of. There are six boxes of tissues in this small room.

A soft knock at the door startles us. We jump to our feet. Disappointingly, it is a staff member with a tray of beverages and light snacks. He seems as stressed as we are and doesn't look like he is more than sixteen.

He's probably a volunteer sent with trays to visiting families. That feels ominous. They don't bring you snacks and drinks to tell you this has been a false alarm, right? To tell you that all is well, and Hattie is being discharged. I manage to croak out a "thank you" to the young man who seems like he can't get away fast enough.

When the door shuts, a gut-wrenching sob escapes. The impact of the last hour is sinking in. I retch into a small wastebasket in the corner of the room. Max holds my hair away from my face and rubs my back until it passes. What has happened? Why aren't we getting any updates? I continue crying into Max's shoulder and realize he, too, is crying. He's never dealt with anything like this before and keeps whispering, "I'm so sorry, I'm so sorry" into my hair.

A flurry of noise erupts from the lobby, and the door whips open with incredible force. Erin flies into the room and throws her arms around us. She, too, is sobbing. Tears had run down the front of her shirt and it's soaking wet. In seconds, the remaining family members have also surrounded us. The warmth and support of their love makes this feel less heavy. We'll hold each other up, no matter what news we get from the doctors. Meg and Sylvie arrive soon after and share hugs with all of us. This feels like an ending, and all of us sense it.

We keep waiting and waiting. Cal goes out to the desk to ask for an update and is told that someone will be with us "soon." The dreaded and timeless "soon." It can make minutes feel like hours and hours like days. There is only so much awkward small talk we can come up with. No one really is up for talking and sharing progress on the house feels wildly inappropriate in this setting. I dig deep but cannot come up with anything to talk about. My mind drifts to the number of tissue boxes in the room, then back to my own well of guilt.

"Is this my fault?" I whisper to Max, returning to a damp day on the water. Hattie covered with blankets, in her hat and coat. When the mist turned to rain, all of us arriving home chilled.

"No, my love. There's no way. Hattie was warm and dry all day, even if the weather was chilly. And there's no way she got sick that fast. Don't blame yesterday for this. It is not your fault," He responds emphatically while shaking his head. He grabs both my hands in his and I see him glance pleadingly at Erin.

"Sweetie, Max is right. She had to have this coming on for a few days. It couldn't have happened that fast.

It must have snuck up on her," she reassures me and puts her arm around me.

I try to find solace in their words, but still, the doubt creeps in. My stomach is in knots, and my hands feel like ice. Maybe I shouldn't have planned a day out on the water for us. The weather has been cooler lately. It probably wasn't the best idea. Even if this wasn't the cause, it may well have been the tipping point.

We request updates two more times. My endlessly patient soon-to-be father-in-law loses his patience with the "soon" answers. At this point, a harried physician and nurse duo join us in the overcrowded room. Introductions are made, Dr. James Ingles and Miranda, the charge nurse for the ER. The Dr and nurse appear startled and slightly annoyed by the number of people present. Cal and Eddie offer their chairs to allow them to sit. Unfazed by the slight scowls, I beg for an update. Impatient from the wait and desperate for news.

Dr. Ingles leans forward, resting his elbows on his knees. Seeming to collect himself, he draws in a slow breath and asks which of us is "the next of kin." With a cold shiver running from the top of my head down, I say, "Me." my voice is quaking, and tears begin falling. Arms wrap around me from both sides.

Max's breathing changes and becomes shallow and tight. Erin quietly starts to cry again. This can't be good.

"When Hattie arrived, she was not breathing on her own. Thankfully, the paramedics had placed the breathing tube before she left home. A few minutes after arrival, her heart did stop." Sobs echo around the small room.

I gasp, and my head drops into my hands. My world feels like it has shifted off its axis. I know the doctor is saying my name, but it sounds like rushing water. I can't make out any words. Max softly and urgently says, "Greer, it's okay. Keep listening." He squeezes my shoulders in support. I nod, trusting that there's something I've missed. It feels like I am hearing him from far away, but I try to refocus.

"Greer— I want to make sure you hear me," Dr. Ingles repeats, "Can you hear me?" I nod and try hard to focus on what he's saying. "Her heart did stop, but we were able to restart it within a few minutes. Because of the breathing tube, she was not overly deprived of oxygen during that time, which is a good thing. Her lungs have too much fluid in them, which is the sound you described to the 911 operator. Between her heart issues and a lung infection that she has probably had for a while, the fluid looks to have built up based on what we've collected. We are admitting her and have started treatment right away for the infection and to decrease the fluid. She will have to stay intubated with the breathing tube for now. Do you have any questions so far?"

A flood of questions pours out: what they think the infection is, how this will affect her heart, which unit she'll be on, and if she's had any other heart attacks. Dr. Ingles answers all of these. The charge nurse, Miranda, goes out to check on Hattie's ICU bed status. She promises to return momentarily.

Before Dr. Ingles leaves, I can't help but ask if I caused this by taking her on the boat. It is weighing on me heavily. He kindly tells me that this is not a new infection but likely has been slowly building over time with the symptoms masked by Hattie's other issues. There is no need to worry that taking Hattie out yesterday contributed to her pneumonia and hospitalization, despite the current circumstances, that brings a minor relief.

Miranda returned with her admission information and asked if we'd like to visit two at a time. Max and I go first with Erin's blessing. She practically pushed us out the door when I asked her if she minded if I went to see Hattie first. On my way out, she stuffed one of the dreadful boxes of tissues at me and gestured to my runny nose with a twinkling smile. It gave me hope that things may not be so bad after all.

Compared to earlier, Hattie does look better. Her skin still has a faint gray tinge, but the color has improved slightly with pink to her lips. The breathing tube is keeping her oxygen levels where they should be. We stand on opposite sides of her bed, each taking a hand. Her skin is cool and clammy, but the feeling of her pulse below my fingertips is reassuring.

She's heavily medicated and doesn't stir. We talk to her all the same. Finding small inconsequential things to share, things she would chat about with us in day-to-day conversation. In that moment, I realized, I never took the pastries out that I was warming up. Knowing she'll appreciate it, I laugh and share this scatter-brained moment with Hattie. Picturing her laughter makes tears well up in my eyes. We say a short prayer with Hattie, tell her how much we love her, and kiss her goodbye. I promise to visit later when she's in her room upstairs. It's time to swap out our visiting spot. One more squeeze to reassure her and me, and then we will take our leave.

Hand in hand, Max and I make our way to the car. What a long and emotionally exhausting day it has been. When he starts the car, we see it is now 11:30 a.m. Our "long day" is not even half over. We'd planned to spend the day doing errands to prep for the wedding. Instead, I'll go back and put the house together and get things ready for another round of days at the hospital.

With a heavy sigh, I lay my head back into the seat of Max's truck. He rests his hand on my thigh, and I encase both of his hands in mine. His hand is comforting and solid. It feels so grounding. He presses his fingers into mine.

Breaking the quiet, I confess, "I couldn't have done today without you."

"I wouldn't have let you. There's no way you should have to face this alone." He grows pensive and focuses on the road in front of us. "Yesterday on the boat, do you remember what you asked me?"

It takes me a second, we'd talked for hours. Then, with a smile, I remember, "Is this what it's going to be like having a husband?"

"Honey, this is what it is going to be like having a husband. You've always had to figure things out and do things by yourself. At least felt like you did. You didn't always have someone to share the good and the bad with. Now you will. That is what having a husband will be." His voice is steady and resolved but filled with so much love.

He turns to face me as we approach the red light, tears shine in his eyes. They match the ones streaming down my face. I take his face in my hands and kiss him until the car behind us honks. Max breaks away and laughs. He waves a thank you and takes off from the light. We both ride along, laughing for several blocks. Our hearts are filled with a mixed bag of emotions—love, happiness, sadness, fear, and peace. I've never felt so many conflicting emotions at once and been okay with it. What a strange journey this is.

Max drops me at the house, collects Brady, and goes to finish some work on the boat. He plans to meet me at the hospital and bring dinner for us. Before I know it, I am alone (except for the dogs). Between the paramedics rushing in and out and our fleeing the house, it is in complete disarray. I decide to start downstairs and work my way up. Hattie's room will take the most work. Putting on good music and pouring a hefty iced coffee will make it go faster and feel less stressful. Erin, Meg, and Sylvie have agreed to update me on Hattie's progress until I return.

Two hours, three iced coffees, and a stale pastry later, the house is in order. Fresh linens are on Hattie's bed, mine too, for good measure. I pushed it too far with the caffeine after all the stress of the morning. Switching to water seems to be a good choice, and I also hope it will dilute some of the caffeine flowing through me.

I take my water to the back porch with the dogs. They seem to have an idea that something has gone on and go to the gate to look over. Soon, the desire to play chase takes over, and they're all running and barking. Drinking the water and watching them play settles me down. My heart feels less like horses galloping in my chest. While they play, I begin a list of items to bring to the hospital. Whether she's awake or not, there are things I know she'll want to have with her. I add these to her list. Favorite socks, a book I can read to her, and a picture of Davis.

With the list complete, heart rate in check, and water consumed, it's time to pack and go to the hospital. Sylvie and Ben have volunteered for dog duty tonight, so the gang will be well cared for while I'm gone. I am unbelievably grateful to be surrounded by people who love us and dive in to help without being asked. Family is not always what you're born into; it's who you have around you.

It has been five days. Hattie is still intubated and giving no indication that she will have the tube taken out any time soon. Her ICU team has been discussing putting in a long-term breathing tube if she doesn't start breathing on her own soon. The infection has decreased, so her heart rate and temperature are better. There is still a decent amount of fluid in her lungs. She has a CT scan this morning, followed by a test to go and look down into her lungs. The doctors are concerned that a new issue may arise. It's not the news we were planning for, but we would all rather know exactly what we're facing. By late afternoon, we will know more.

My phone rings around lunch, and it is a local number, though not saved in my contacts. The anxiety and excitement of an unknown number is a remnant of my youth when the house phone would ring. I hesitantly answer to be met with loud squawking and a load of background noise. Immediately, I knew who it was. A friend of Hattie's who runs a local animal rescue. She's calling to get an update but has lost her phone and has borrowed one from her new volunteer. These calls roll in throughout the day on Hattie's phone and mine. I give a generic update and ask if she can share with their friend group since we'll be out of the room and unable to take calls. She promises to share and disconnects.

These are the small stories that I share with Hattie throughout our days together. I keep her up to date on her friends and who has called. The team keeps assuring us that she can hear everything we say, so we keep talking and telling stories during each visit. We hope she hears us and keeps fighting. Selfishly, I need her to rally and wake up. My wedding is less than a month away. She has to be there to be a part of our day.

Good news! The tests showed no new diseases or tumors in Hattie's lungs. Her scan shows that the fluid has diminished since she was admitted. While still present, it is showing signs of improvement. All positive news! The respiratory team turned down some ventilator settings, which also means she's improving. We had mini celebrations in her room, two at a time this evening, complete with music and balloons. Erin and Kayla brought in cupcakes and muffins for the staff as a thank-you. Every day we are in awe of the work they do and how graciously they care for patients and families.

While I sit with Hattie, I also work on minor wedding details that need to be finalized. We did our final cake tasting Monday evening when Max finished his charters. I tell Hattie the details of our cake selection. Vanilla bean with a raspberry filling, the cake topper will be our initials in gold, fresh camellia blossoms, and tendrils of ivy. No plastic bride and groom for us! Although there were some adorable choices available. Flower deliveries have been confirmed by email and are set to be dropped off at the café on Wednesday before the wedding. We are storing the flowers in the large fridges in the back storage area. We will assemble bouquets and boutonnieres that Thursday to give the blossoms time to open.

My dress has arrived, and the final fitting is next Tuesday, which reminds me to lay off sitting and mindlessly eating all the treats folks keep bringing. I have to zip that dress up and there is little margin for extra cupcakes. Bridesmaid dresses have arrived, fit checks done, and are at the cleaners to be steamed. Tuxes will be picked up the week of the wedding on Thursday when Max and I got to pick up Joel and Janine at the airport. Hattie has been subjected to my to-do lists and calendar updates for days. She's going to wake up reciting it.

I wake up in the pre-dawn hours to my cell and the house phone ringing, which incites a heart-stuttering panic. Obviously, something has happened to Hattie. I grab my cell phone off the night table. Fumbling with it and frustrating myself, I answer in a huff, "Hello, is she OK?"

"SHE'S AWAKE!" Meg screams into the phone. I jump from the bed and start rushing to grab clothes. Meg sketches out the details for me. I switch the phone to speakerphone while I throw on leggings and a sweatshirt.

"The night nurse noticed a change in Hattie's vital signs and reduced her sedation overnight. They got orders to keep reducing it. The doctor decided to trial turning it off this morning during his 6 am rounds. Within a few minutes, Hattie had her eyes open. She responds to questions by squeezing her hands and blinking her eyes. For now, she is breathing around her breathing tube. After another hour or so of that, they'll try to take it. Get here as soon as you can!"

I rush through breakfast with the dogs, pour myself an XL iced coffee, and grab a bagel. The dogs do their morning rounds in record time and are back inside for treats. I am out the door twenty minutes after Meg's call and seem reasonably put together, at least to myself. For all I know, I look like a maniac. I'm just glad

I took the time to wash my face and brush my teeth.
Don't want to scare Hattie.

Chapter Thirteen

♥

-Hattie-

I have no idea what has happened. Over the course of the last several hours, I feel like I have woken up from the longest and worst night's sleep of my life. Everyone has been in my dreams, and they have talked non-stop about everything under the sun. My memories of what they were saying are fuzzy for now. Actually, everything is fuzzy. What I know for sure is that I am stiff as a board, my hands don't seem to lift when I try, my lips are dry, and my throat is so sore. Something is in my throat, and I can't talk.

Meg is beside me and highly excited. She's on the phone with different people and talking loudly. I am having trouble understanding exactly what she's say-ing. A short while later, the room has several doctors, nurses, and respiratory staff. So many people are staring at me. I can now assume I am in the hospital. Greer is now beside me, holding my hand. She kisses my forehead and tells me how glad she is to see me awake.

The doctors talk with her and tell her they think, "I'm ready." Ready for what? I squeeze her hand frantically and widen my eyes. Greer looks at me and explains that I have a breathing tube that the doctors will need to take out. I shake my head vigorously. My throat hurts so badly, and I don't know if I'll be able to stand them pulling anything from my throat. Greer asks if it will be painful. "Will what be painful?" The team explains how they'll make it comfortable for me.

Despite their reassurances, I am still scared. This morning has been a lot. Tears begin to stream down my face even though I cannot make a sound. Greer and Meg stroke my face and hands. Greer takes the doctor aside and talks with them. She returns to my bedside with the doctor. He explains slowly and carefully what will happen, again how they will keep me comfortable, and the instructions to follow, and ends by asking if I am ready. Whether I am or not, I nod vigorously—no time like the present. I still don't fully understand what we're about to do, but I'd rather they do it and have it over with.

An hour later, after a breathing treatment that helped soothe my throat, I am sucking on some delicious ice chips. Hands down, it's the best thing I have had in a long time. Literally, it has been ten days since I last ate. My cough interrupts things fairly frequently, and I can't really talk, but I am breathing on my own.

Removing the tube was far smoother than what I had pictured, and I was glad we got it over and done with. This is going to take a while for me to wrap my brain around all that has gone on and how I got here. In bits and pieces, I am hearing about pneumonia and fluid in my lungs, which would explain the cough. In between visitors, I need to sleep. Not just in the "could use a nap," more of a "couldn't stay awake if I tried."

During one of these breaks, I wake to a dark, empty room. I can't say that I am sad. Today has been overwhelming, and I need the time to rest mentally and physically. No matter how tired I am, I drift off thinking that I'm immensely grateful for the outpouring of love and support.

Over the coming days, my memories become slightly clearer. I don't have any of the day I came in or the ambulance coming to the house. I remember being so tired and asking Greer to save me some supper. Then, the dreams of everyone talking with me and waking up with a sore throat. I am able to recall some of what was said, but the timeline is off, and it doesn't make much sense. What has become very clear to me is that I am forever changed by this. From here on, I won't "get better" to the level everyone hopes I will. This episode has taken a considerable chunk from my strength reserves. What remained of them anyway.

-Greer-

Hattie has been in the hospital for nearly three weeks and is finally coming home! She will be on oxygen all the time, and we'll make some modifications to the house for it to be more navigable for her. I talked about which room she'd prefer before we began. She does not want to take the stairs, "I don't have the breath for it."

It was decided to use the dining room as a new bedroom space. She's always treasured her dining room, saving it for special occasions. Davis and Hattie used to throw phenomenal dinner parties for his colleagues. The 12-person table would be laid beautifully with a rotation of dinnerware and place settings kept in an antique hutch from the early 1900s. She carefully chose each color, texture, and piece in this room. The walls are papered in an ivory damask with soft white semi-gloss wainscoting. You'd think the two wouldn't go well, but the shimmering white in the damask paper matches with the glossy paint below. A chandelier hangs over the table; throughout the years, she's updated it to keep it from appearing dated. It's currently a tiered brass eight-light chandelier with thin shell accents that reflects the light back softly—one of those rooms you find yourself staring into but not wanting to touch.

We called for an all-hands-on-deck in the group chat. This afternoon, we kicked it off. First things first, we emptied the dining room, carefully packing away the table settings that were always in place. After all, no Southern woman would leave her table unprepared, and Hattie is no exception. She is forever ready for a party, formal or informal.

Kayla, Lauren, Sarah, and I are on wrapping duty. Who knew that practice packing months ago would be put to use again so soon? Meg and Erin assemble boxes and place items inside. Sylvie carefully labels each then Ben, Seth, and Eddie carry them to the box truck.

Sylvie and Ben have brought their box truck and are providing a space in their warehouse for us to place Hattie's dining room items. They've also contributed an antique wardrobe since there will be no closet in the dining room. Bless them for thinking of it! Max and Cal are disassembling the furniture and wrapping the hutch and sideboard for storage. It takes us about three hours to entirely empty and pack the dining room. Meg leaves for her visitation shift with Hattie while we tromp upstairs to move the bedroom furniture and items downstairs.

Over the last few days, I'd preemptively packed most of Hattie's clothes and small items. We'd known she was coming home, and this was on the horizon. Turns out this has saved us a significant amount of time. Hattie's antique bedroom suite was a wedding gift from Davis. The king-sized sleigh bed is a gleaming mahogany with a matching dresser, a large carved mirror, and nightstands. She's lovingly polished it weekly for as long as I can remember. I've always loved helping her and the feel of the glossy, cool wood.

Before we start taking her furniture from her room, I take a few minutes alone, savoring the space. The rest of our group has taken a break on the porch. This moment feels like a part of saying goodbye to Hattie.

She won't be sleeping in this room anymore. The space she and Davis shared for decades will no longer be theirs. One so filled with love will now be an empty room. It hurts, and I am glad Hattie is not here to help with this.

By the time everyone rejoins me, I am sitting next to the bed, collecting items from the nightstand tops. We will carry them downstairs without opening the drawers. It feels too invasive to go through them and is entirely unnecessary. They are heavy and bulky, but by wrapping them in blankets, each safely makes it to the dining room. We strip the bed and carefully disassemble the frame keeping track of the screws. One of Hattie's conditions was that she not be placed in a hospital bed on her return home. It may have its challenges, but we will make sure she has her comfortable and familiar bed. This round, there is little to be boxed up. Sylvie switches out visiting with Meg and takes Seth to spend time with Hattie.

By dinner time, the dining room has been converted into a cozy bedroom space. We stand back and are pleased with our work. While it does seem a bit odd to see it as a bedroom now, it feels like we've done our best to give Hattie a restful space to recover in. The doorbell rings, and dinner arrives; I wasn't even aware it had been ordered. Apparently, someone had taken care of it, and I'm delighted they thought of it. We're all exhausted but happy with what we were able to accomplish. Now, to bring Hattie home.

-Hattie-

We made it home around just before lunch, and the transformation of the dining room blew me away. I'd honestly envisioned just moving things aside for me. There was no need to make a fuss. Instead, the space has been made into a cozy bedroom with everything that comforts me. There are so many thoughtful touches sprinkled throughout the room. New curtains were hung to block the light and allow me to rest. A folding screen hides away the medical equipment, so I don't have it in my line of sight all day. The stunning wardrobe from Sylvie and Ben's shop that I've had my eye on holds a selection of my hanging winter clothes. I credit Greer and Erin for making those choices, all my go-to favorites.

After lunch, I need to nap. When Greer closes the solid pine pocket doors, I am tucked away in a quiet space all my own. Tears fill my eyes. I had not expected this at all. The amount of love from these people never ceases to amaze me.

–Greer–

Hattie has finally come home! Nestling her into her big bed this afternoon for a nap, I could not stop smiling. I am sure I would have looked unbalanced to anyone else, but Hattie had the same expression on her face. She was delighted with her "new" bedroom and felt so peaceful. We did talk about adding a little table and chair in case she doesn't feel up to coming out to the kitchen or porch for a meal. This will make it even easier for her to recoup her strength. She said she is committed to being outside with us for the wedding in two weeks and wants to save up what she can.

Our next day will be filled with home care staff coming by to finish setting up, and we are unbelievably grateful for all the support. Hattie has come home with an astounding amount of medications and new breathing treatments. She will remain on oxygen full-time. We can easily adjust, but having that additional assistance while we transition to this new phase will be extremely helpful. A Nurse Practitioner is scheduled to visit her to save her from traveling out for her follow-up appointments.

The home care nurse (Phoebe) came with a physical therapist (Therea) and a social worker (Alice). They were armed with instructions, equipment, and plans to help Hattie regain strength and adjust to her new routines. Both of us immediately felt like we were fast friends with the whole team. This was a special group of women who, no doubt, are experts at bonding quickly with their patients and families. Alice helped me with billing questions and determining additional resources available through Hattie's insurance. She also went over the importance of planning for the future, and when Hattie's health worsens, her honesty is both surprising and refreshing. We need to keep those doses of reality in with our hope.

While we chatted, Phoebe and Theresa got Hattie up and walking to the bathroom. It may not be very far, but Hattie said, "Was that a mile?" when she returned to her chair. This made us all giggle and put in perspective that Hattie has not had much activity for nearly a month. We learned transferring techniques, stretches, and exercises. Phoebe went over medication schedules and filled the weekly pill box. We were shocked that we spent more than four hours with them! Hattie mentioned my wedding in two weeks and honeymoon during her time with the team. We started a binder with printouts of instructions, schedules, exercises, and tips at their recommendation. This will help when we have others helping us in the next few weeks. Hattie and I came away feeling so much better and ready to tackle our latest adventure together.

Chapter Fourteen

♥

-Greer-

That first week home was a doozy! Trying to figure out timing and schedules took both of our brainpower, but we made it through. By the first Sunday home, it feels like we've got it. I get up and make coffee for us both—regular for me and decaf for Hattie. We never thought we'd see the day she asked for decaf. She made the switch while in the hospital out of necessity and has stuck with it.

I'd made a veggie, bacon quiche, and fruit salad for a relaxed morning at home. It's quickly plated and carried to the porch. Hattie and I easily transfer her to the wheelchair and out onto the back porch- we're so proud of ourselves that we salute and give a high five, dissolving into giggles. She's bundled to the hilt and so happy to be out here eating. We chat about the week ahead. The wedding is six days away, and there is so much to do but nothing significant left to do.

"I want us to be able to enjoy these next few days. We're on the edge of a major change and I want to savor every moment," I tell Hattie between bites.

She's in the process of twisting her hair up into a clip and distractedly answers, "I agree. You two should enjoy every step." I pause with my fork held in the air and realize I must be staring. "There's nothing wrong with it, sweetie. You should."

"Hattie– I meant you and me," I say and begin to cackle. I mean yes, I do plan to enjoy my time with Max, but I really meant I want to focus on spending some time with Hattie. She tips her head back laughing and it delights me to see her relaxed. The hair she was so diligently working on twisting falls back out of the clip, and she tosses it on the table. Her chestnut hair may have more sparkles of gray than a few years ago, but it is still beautiful and thick. I stand and clip it up for her. She pats my hand when I'm done, and we resume eating.

"Hey, Greer! Your phone is going crazy," Hattie calls from the porch. I'd gone to take our plates in and refill coffees. The process takes slightly longer now that I have to keep track of which is which.

"Can you see who it is?" I crack the window and ask. Figuring it must be urgent if the calls and texts are back-to-back this early on a Sunday.

"It's Joel..." Hattie says without finishing. That sounds ominous. The tone of her voice tells me something is going on. She's also never really pleased to hear from him. I tell her a quick "One sec" and finish as quickly as I can in the kitchen.

I have two missed calls and eight text messages from Joel and Janine. I start with the text thread.

Janine: *"Happy wedding week! Joel and I are so excited for you."*

Joel: *"Greer— we woke up to a huge snowstorm that came in overnight. It isn't looking good in the mountains."*

Janine: *"What your father means is the mountain passes have tons of snow on them. It could make travel difficult."*

Joel: *"Yes. That's what I meant. The roads are impassable as of now."*

Janine: *"Please don't be negative, dear. There's a good chance it will clear."*

Joel: *"I want to be honest with her. We might not get down off the mountain and I don't want to spring it on her last minute."*

Janine: *"Joel, she can see these messages."*

Joel: *"Oh, sorry, honey. I want you to be prepared in case we can't travel. Call us when you can."*

Don't you love group messages? I sigh and read the exchange to Hattie. She shakes her head and says, "You call, I'll check the weather." Before I call, I send a quick text to Max with screenshots of the text thread. He replies with a horrified face emoji and says, *"I'll be there soon."*

I tap on Joel's number, but there is no answer. Janine's is the same. I try the house phone and get a busy tone. Assuming they may be on the phone, I send a text to call when they can.

The relaxed feeling I've had all morning is now replaced by tension. Hattie suggests I take a hot shower while we wait for Joel and Janine to return the call. That does sound like a far better plan than sitting and stewing. On our way into the house, we decide not to spend the day worrying about it. The weather is beyond our control. Hattie wants to stay in the kitchen and go through the mail. I settle her, and get her all the beverages she could ask for, then go upstairs to stew in the shower instead of on the porch.

The moment I open my door, I hear Max and Hattie in the kitchen. Their easy conversation and Max's low, rumbling laugh float up the stairs. Part of me wants to return to my room, letting them have time with one another. It slips my mind sometimes that Hattie has always been a part of Max's life. She was there the day he was born and has been involved in every milestone of his life, right there with his family. He loves her as much as I do. Realizing my hair is still a bit too damp and looking for an excuse to give them a few extra minutes, I softly close my door and turn to find my blow dryer.

Hair fully dry, I make my way down to a quiet kitchen. Max sits alone with an empty plate and a cooling cup of coffee. He's reading a magazine and looks up when I enter. A broad smile creases his face, it reaches all the way into his golden-brown eyes. He stands and wraps me in a hug, asking if I'm ok. I'm not, and we both know it.

Having my father at the wedding was already complicated. I'd come to a sort of peace with it. Now that it has been disrupted, I am relieved at the thought that he may not be there. Which, in the same heartbeat, makes me feel tremendously guilty. He isn't a bad person; he's never mistreated me; he just has never been a part of my life, always on the periphery and by his own choosing. There was a phase after graduation when I tried so hard, but he was happy with the way things were. And that sucked big time. It hurt and made me realize that I am ok with him having and keeping his space. Not everyone is meant to be a parent.

Instead of saying all this, I sigh heavily and say, "I will be."

Max kisses the top of my head and releases me, knowing full well that I desperately need more coffee. Hattie has headed back to bed to rest for a bit. Max and I pour to-go cups of coffee and take as many dogs as will go for a walk. It may be December, but life by the beach means there is usually warm enough weather for a walk outside.

We cut through the neighborhoods and ended up at our favorite beach spot. Max throws sticks endlessly for the dogs while we walk the shoreline. This is what I needed: time to focus on what and who I love. Sneaking up behind Max, I snag him around the waist and whisper, "Six days, my love," into his back. He wraps his hands around mine, and we intertwine our fingers. We stand together, taking a few minutes to breathe deeply in sync, watching the dogs play.

"Hey lovebirds!" rings out loudly down the beach. We turn to see Ben and Sylvie walking toward us hand in hand.

"Same to you," I say, smiling. They're still so cute after forty-three years of marriage. I hope we are that sweet still in 40+ years.

They join us, and we walk together for a bit. Sylvie wants to know every minute detail of the wedding plans for the week. Ben wants to hear about the progress of the house and land. We could honestly talk for hours with them. I want to hear about the impending arrival of their latest grandbaby. This will be grandbaby number nine and Sylvie is just as excited as she was with the first. Sylvie and Ben have four children. Their oldest son is about ten years older than us, and their youngest is a few years younger. All of their kids are married with children. When the family visits, it is a full house, one that is packed with love and laughter. It's so fun to spend time with them. We make plans to get together when they're back from their trip up north, and we're back from the honeymoon. They split off to open the shop for weekend visitors, and we decided to walk back home.

On the way, my phone starts ringing, catching us both off guard. It is nearly always on silent. I scramble to find it in my pocket and answer without looking at the screen.

"Greer? Is that you? It's crackling and hard to hear." Janine's voice comes through in a weird staccato pattern. Clearly, the connection isn't great; I answer that it's me and turn my phone to check my bars. I've got full service. I shrug and put it on speaker.

"Are you guys okay?" I ask Janine, genuinely concerned about all the snow and that I haven't heard back from them.

"We're fine, dear. Your father insisted we try to plow out the driveway. The snow is pounding down with no signs of slowing. We didn't make much progress...." her voice trails off in disappointment. She had been looking forward to coming. Janine has always stayed in better contact with me than Joel has, and I have a soft spot for her.

"How's it looking?" I ask tentatively. I'm relatively sure I know the answer.

"Not good. Not good at all. The weather service is calling for two more days of snow like this. The mountain will be completely impassable. Had we known how bad it would be, we would have left last week. I am so sorry, my dear." Janine's voice cracks with the apology.

Tears now sting my eyes, hearing the sadness in Janine's voice. She's called me because Joel isn't good at these conversations. "I know you would have." Sniffling, I try to find a tissue. Bless Max, he wipes my face with his sleeve.

"Your father won't ever tell you this; he's outside, and that's what I called. It meant the world to him that you wanted him to be involved in your wedding. He never expected you to offer him to walk you down the aisle. He's the first to admit that he didn't act like a father to you at any point in your life." Janine is now crying openly. I had no idea how he felt all these years. My bratty bad behavior makes me feel even worse, and it should. I realize I did want them at the wedding. Whether he gave me away or not, I wanted them there. "He's out punishing the driveway and snowdrifts, taking it out on them. I promise you that if there is any way for us to be there, we will. But I don't want to give you false hope."

I thank her. She hasn't only given me an update, but she's also shared a glimpse into how Joel really feels. She makes another assurance to keep me up to date and disconnects with, "We love you, Greer." I mumble, "Love you too."

Standing and staring at my phone, Max and I are silent. We start walking toward the house slowly while I think about the conversation. I finally say, "They haven't said that in years." Janine had said it with such genuineness that I knew she meant it.

On our arrival at the house, I knock gently on Hattie's bedroom door. It's answered with a low woof from Sadie and a smiling "hello" from Hattie. She's sitting in her chair by the window. Clearly proud of herself for getting out of bed and into her chair without help, she gestures to her chair like she's in a gameshow. We celebrate her strength beginning to return. She joins us in the kitchen, ambling down the hall with Max and me on either side.

While I prep lunch, Max and Hattie work on party favors for our small number of guests. Tying fisherman's knots around the small bottles with sand and mini seashells. Our initials and the wedding date are in gold on the front. We tell Hattie about the call with Janine and her revelations. Hattie is as surprised as I am, responding, "Will wonders never cease."

I don't want her to feel pressured to escort me down the aisle, so I don't say anything. I am happy enough for her to give me away at the end. Having her be any part means the world to us. We discuss other parts of the ceremony and a few loose ends.

Max whips his head up and stares like a deer in headlights. I freeze and feel inexplicably panicky. A nervous sweat whips up. "What? What is it?"

"Vows. Have you written your vows?" he asks. A look of "please say you haven't yet because I haven't" on his face.

"Oh yeah, weeks ago. Why? Have you not started?" I ask with my face in a mask of sanctimonious blandness. His face blanches. Recognizing I am full of nonsense and haven't started either, he tosses a mini shell in my direction. I am adding vows to our list for the week. We agree to have them ready by the rehearsal on Friday night.

Sarah and Meg knock on the back door, and Hattie waves them in. The smell of freshly baked cookies wafts in with them. Sarah has been working on chocolate peanut butter brookies and iced oatmeal cookies. We gladly have a sample of each. Her baking skills have greatly improved. This summer, she plans to work for the local bakery that supplies Erin's café to learn more skills and techniques. She offered to make our treats for the rehearsal dinner, and I was delighted to include her! She's tested dozens of cookies and mini fruit tarts.

Meg takes Hattie's spot, tying the fisherman's knots on the few remaining favors as we sit and chat. Sarah and Meg agree to join us for lunch. We pass the afternoon relaxing and enjoying one another's company. Another sweet memory to add to my bank.

Max and "the guys" are going out for dinner and to the shooting range tonight. We're having a ladies night at the house to celebrate my last weekend as a single lady. This weekend has snuck up on all of us! I was feeling unprepared, but thank goodness I have friends who are happy to have a relaxed night with wine, pizza, and a myriad of tiny appetizers.

During Hattie's hospitalization, I went through an appetizer phase. I became obsessed with ones that could be frozen and pulled out in batches when needed. Tonight, we are reaping the benefits of those sleepless nights. On platters, we have mini quiches, savory meatballs in a creamy sauce, potato and cheese pierogis, Korean dumplings, half-sized empanadas, spicy crab pinwheels, and croquettes—a mix with something for everyone. I send Max out the door with a few treats on a paper plate despite him begging to be allowed to stay. The closer the wedding gets, the harder it is to kick him out.

My favorite thing is hearing how people met their spouse or significant other. It usually takes little prompting to hear the stories. I am the most familiar with Hattie and Davis. But I still am happy to hear of the love-struck Hattie falling for her best friend's "devilishly handsome" older brother when he came home from college. She has always described him the same way and how she felt when they crossed paths that summer. They both knew they were done for.

Erin and Cal's story is less familiar to me. They'd met at an event hosted by Erin's parents. Their fathers were colleagues. Erin was twenty and Cal was twenty-two. She thought he had kind eyes but was in a no-dating phase. They danced and chatted, then parted ways. A few months later, they met again at another event and hit it off. Erin reluctantly agreed to a date. They married within a year. Erin says, "he was smitten from day one; it took me a couple of extra days," and then winks at me.

Sylvie shares her story and says that it's "a little less romantic." She and Ben were raised in the same neighborhood and attended different schools, but their families were always connected. During their freshman year of high school, they started dating. On her graduation night, he proposed. They married six months later and had their first son "9 months and 21 days" later. The rest she says, "is history," and then laughs.

Meg shares the story of meeting her ex-husband. She was waitressing at a local diner, and he would come in after work one or two nights a week. Night after night, he was assigned to her section. One night, she found out he was asking to be seated there. She says that while it may not have ended well, they had some pleasant years, and she got her beautiful babies from it. Then, she shares about meeting a new fellow recently and that they've been casually seeing each other for about six weeks. We all pepper her with questions and insist she bring him as her plus one to the wedding. She glows when she talks about him, and we cannot wait to meet him! Meg deserves a fresh start.

Surf tells us about the first time she met Jimmy on a diving trip with Lauren. He was with a group of friends who were all showing off. She'd thought he was a complete dweeb. Throughout the week, they got to talk and spend time in the water, and she was impressed by his skill as a diver and his knowledge of the oceans. When the trip was wrapping up, he asked for her number so he could stay in touch. They dated over the next two years, mainly long-distance, due to his job on offshore rigs. Their wedding was so lovely and true to who they are.

Kayla and Eddie were high school friends but never dated. They spent time with the same friend groups and enjoyed each other's company. A chance meeting after college in town sparked an interest, and then Eddie helped with some odd jobs at her house. They spent more and more time together and started dating within a couple of months. In less than a year, they were married. That was four years ago, and now they've got baby number two on the way.

Lauren laughs and says her prince is still out there, but she is accepting applications. Sarah's face reddens when we look at her. She says, "No way!" and makes herself busy helping with food refills in the kitchen.

The remainder of the night is spent telling stories and laughing at ridiculous moments over the years. How different this year is ending than how it began!

Chapter Fifteen

♥

-Hattie-

Joel and Janine called last night. They're officially snowed in with no hope of getting out for their flight tomorrow. Which means they won't make it to the wedding. We plan to have Ben video-call them to make sure they're a part of the ceremony. How many video weddings did we all go through during the pandemic? It will give a nostalgic feel like the old days with someone on a video call during the ceremony. Hopefully, we're all a little better at it than we used to be.

Greer took the news worse than either of us thought she would. Her big emotions caught her off guard, and she was embarrassed by them. We spent a good deal of time on the porch talking about how she feels now and how it relates to how she grew up. There will always be that little girl who wants her daddy to be involved, even if she acts like she doesn't. By the end of the chat, she was feeling better and ready to take on the week. Sometimes, you need to accept how you feel in the moment, talk about it, spend time with it, and then move on.

The wedding is only three days away, and I am tickled pink. A month ago, it didn't look like I would be here for this. Yet here I am. Greer doesn't know that I've been working with Theresa every chance I get. We've been doing extra exercises to get my strength back. Even before the call from Janine, there was something that told me it wouldn't work out with her father. Today, I could walk from my bedroom all the way out onto the porch—a much further distance than I'll need. We even did a sneaky test run and added onto my oxygen tubing. But we've got a plan for that. I've enlisted Seth as my helper. He's always willing to jump in, mainly when he thinks it is some sort of shenanigans.

All the flowers arrived at Erin's café this morning. We've spent the last couple of evenings making backings for boutonnieres and corsages, tying ribbons that will be placed on chairs, and getting the decorations ready. The sweetest thing was a flower crown for baby

Annabelle. I know everyone calls her Annie for short. But I love to use her full name to honor our beloved Annabelle. Kayla and Eddie will walk down the aisle with Annabelle between them.

Cal and Eddie came over last night with a stunning wooden arch they made for Max and Greer to stand beneath during the ceremony. It was a surprise gift—such a loving and thoughtful touch. Greer and Max plan to incorporate it into the new house somehow. We have flowers, vines, and twinkling lights to decorate it with. The wedding vendor will deliver chairs on Friday morning, but we won't set them up until the wedding day. Just in case we have some wet weather move in. The forecast shows rain tonight and tomorrow, but it is all clear as of Friday. It's December; the weather is unpredictable out here. Nearly everything is coming together beautifully for them, and I cannot wait for Saturday. My precious girl is getting married!

–Greer–

How is it already Friday? This week has flown at a pace that doesn't seem real. It's like we have entered a time vortex. So many things have happened and seem to be falling into place. Other than Joel and Janine not making the wedding, it all feels on track, which terrifies me to say—cause, you know, Murphy's Law and all that. Today, I am committed to thinking positively! I AM GETTING MARRIED TOMORROW!!

The day blurs past me. Manicures and pedicures with Hattie, Erin, Kayla, Lauren, and Surf. Lunch at the Hickory Dickory café on the dock. Home to rest for a bit and make sure Hattie feels well enough for the rehearsal dinner. We've all tried to be super cautious with her this last week. We don't want her getting too tired and having a turn before the wedding. So far, so good.

While Hattie napped, I decided to pack my bag for the honeymoon. Why I have waited until now is beyond me. In all the excitement for the week, packing a bag has fallen off my radar. Also, having no idea where we are going has slightly altered my ability to pack. Max told me I should plan to be warm, and that's all I'm getting out of him. Truth be told, it's a honeymoon. How much do I need to pack? Surprises are fantastic but also majorly stressful.

The good news is that I can spend hours packing since the rehearsal is at the house—no need to worry about getting ready and driving to another location.

We'll have some of the sweets Sarah made to snack on during the rehearsal. Then, head to the Anchor for our family dinner after we finish.

Hattie calls up the stairs a few hours later to check on me. I was out like a light. Having packed what I thought I'd need, minus toiletries and chargers, I'd gone through my substantial to-be-read stack by the bed to select a few for the trip. I fell asleep while reading. I guess that one can stay home, it clearly is not going to hold my attention. After rubbing the sleep from my eyes and, in the process, smearing makeup all over my face, I tell Hattie I'll wash up and be right down.

We sit together on the porch. Most of the furniture has been put away in the garage or basement. The porch feels barren, and I wonder if we'll be able to get it all put back after the wedding. Hattie pipes up that the porch "Feels naked," which prompts a round of giggling.

Max texts that he's on his way. He's nervous and wants to get ready here instead of at his parent's house. It is sweet that he needs to be here to be calm. I leave Hattie on the porch with the dogs while I go in to make tea. The weather is a little chilly, and thankfully, the rain has stopped. Tea will help settle my nerves and keep us both warm. Hattie suggests I put a little whiskey in mine and make one for Max. I consider this seriously but feel I should offer it to him first. As I carry the tea to the porch, I hear the front door unlock and smile, knowing Max has arrived.

"Be right back," I tell Hattie and rush back inside. I fling myself at him. He lifts me off the ground and buries his face in my hair. He smells like salty air and boat fuel. It is a combination that I am a super fan of, but I recognize it is an acquired taste. I snuggle against his neck, realizing this was the last day of our lives we'd have to spend apart.

"Why am I more nervous for this doggone rehearsal than I am for our wedding tomorrow?" he asks me, his voice still muffled as he sets my feet on the floor. He was still pressing his face into my hair.

"You mean you don't love walking back and forth in front of people and having them critique it?" I respond, trying to lessen his nerves. "Hattie did suggest putting whiskey in our tea to calm us down. Want some?"

"Nah. I'll take the tea and a hot shower. I'm sure I smell like the boat. An engine was smoking this morn-ing, I had to get it fixed before the wedding."

"You do have that man of the sea smell. But you know I love it. You hit the shower, and I'll restart the kettle. Join us on the porch when you're all clean."

With a parting smooch, he jogs for the stairs, and I back to making tea before rejoining Hattie.

Soon, the house is full of family and friends, all chatting happily and snacking. Once the officiant arrives, we get this party started. Tape is laid on the porch for the aisle we'll walk down. A soft runner with the colors of our wedding- sage, deep blues, and ivory- will replace the tape tomorrow. The exquisite arch stands at the end of the porch. The officiant will stand in the center with Max and I. The wedding party will be fanned out on either side.

We did away with bride and groom seating for those in attendance. Nearly everyone coming knows both of us. We discuss the ceremony logistics, and then it is time to practice. I'm suddenly so nervous that my palms are sweaty, and my heart thuds. I rub my hands on my pant legs to dry them and spy Max doing a similar move. We swap nervous glances, and he pulls a face that makes us both smile. It helps to relieve some of the tension. My God, I love that man.

Walking alone down the aisle toward Max, I am swamped with emotions. Hattie calls them my "big emotions," the ones that matter in life. My heart is so full of love that it practically burns in my chest, feeling like it has expanded beyond what my ribs can hold in.

I struggle to walk to the pace of the music and am reminded that I need to walk, not jog, down the aisle, much to the delight of all present. With a "cut it out" from Hattie, everyone reigns it in, and we can focus.

After several practice runs, we have prepped all we can for tomorrow. Neither of us is less nervous, but continuing to practice hasn't seemed to help. This is a lot for someone who has never loved sharing emotions or being the center of attention. Max and I take a few quiet minutes on the porch after the others have gone in. We both are still sweaty palmed, and wound up, but sitting together in the chilly air is the reset we need. Heads clearer and nerves calmer, we rejoin our families inside. With dinner reservations at 7:30, we won't have much time to spare if we don't get a move on.

-Hattie-

When we get home from the rehearsal dinner, I ask Max and Greer to join me in the kitchen for a few minutes. I want to give them their gift tonight instead of waiting until tomorrow. I've always planned to do it for Greer, and tonight feels like the proper night.

We settle around the table, and I rummage around in the large leather tote I've brought from the bedroom. I withdraw two file folders, a large manilla envelope, and a wrapped gift box. Both of them have pleasantly confused looks on their faces but sit patiently while I get everything ready. I sigh deeply and begin. Placing my palm on the gift box first, I slowly slide it to the center of the table but keep my hand resting on the top.

"I am so proud of you two and so happy for you. You're on the start of your new life together. Davis and I made arrangements many years ago to give Greer a wedding gift. He would be thrilled to know the two of you are marrying. He has loved you like family since birth, Max. He'd be delighted to see you're making it official. Even though he isn't with me physically today, he's still a part of this." I start the conversation out, "Greer, you were the daughter we always wanted but never got. First, I want you to open this, and I'll explain it." I slide the box across the table and release my hand.

Greer looks at me with a puzzled expression and reaches for the box, positioning it between herself and Max. They open the box to see three small boxes—one of them is an antique jewelry box. I am genuinely curious to see which they pick first, for no reason in particular.

They remove them and line them up on the table. Greer suggests that Max choose the first box. He selects the middle box. On opening, they find a ring of keys. Max plucks the keys out; after a quick glance at one another, they turn to look at me in unison.

"Davis and I deeded the house and property to Greer the year before he passed. These are the keys to the house and garage. It has been yours for years, but we make it official today."

Greer gasps and covers her mouth with her hands, clearly shocked by this news. "I had no idea you'd done that. Thank you so much. I've always loved this house." Max appears to be equally stunned and sits with his mouth slightly agape.

"You'll notice there seem to be more keys than necessary." I gesture at the ring containing different keys. Both nod, with their eyes slightly bulged.

"With Davis's business, we have acquired several income properties over the years; some are homes, but two are business spaces in town. These have also been deeded to you as well. One of which is the gallery." Another gasp, this one from Max.

"Would you like to open another box?" I ask and gesture to the remaining two boxes. They nod, and Greer selects the smaller box.

Flipping open a lid reveals a short, oddly shaped key. "That is a key to a safe deposit box at the bank. We kept most of our valuables-jewelry, bonds, family treasures, and emergency cash in the box. The contents have been signed over to you." I look at their faces, and it appears that their eyes cannot get much bigger. "Take a few breaths, and let's open the last one."

They hold it between them, and Max quietly opens the lid. Inside are Davis and I's wedding rings and my engagement ring. I'd switched to wearing a diamond anniversary band only years ago, putting these away for safekeeping. Tears spill from Greer's eyes, and a quiet sob escapes. Max wraps his arm around her, and they lean their heads together. Pausing for a moment to take it all in. I give them a minute and then slide the folders and envelope across the table.

"The folders contain the paperwork on the properties. There isn't anything you'll need to do. I've taken care of it all with our lawyer. The envelope has family photos that have been passed around for generations that I thought you'd like to have."

Greer glides out of her seat and across the table to me. Throwing her arms around me next. She's crying and thanking me. She's joined by Max, who tucks us into a hug and thanks me. More will come after my death, but I wanted to give them this on a happy occasion.

They retake their seats, and we open the envelope of photos. We talk through the memories Greer has in some of them, and I explain who is in the older photos. It's a relaxed way to end the conversation. Before we know it, the living room clock chimes 11. We decide to call it a night. After a lovely and sappy send-off for Max, Greer and I make our tea and head to our rooms. Tomorrow is the big day, and I am delighted to be a part of it.

Chapter Sixteen

♥

–Greer–

Decomposember has come through for us with today's weather. We woke up to one of those perfect southern winter days. I've been in fear of horrendous storms moving in and a ridiculous cold front. It will be in the low 60s and sunny by this afternoon. It's a little chilly but by no means cold. I couldn't ask for better weather at an outdoor wedding.

The house is a swirl of activity right away. I came down at 8 a.m., and there were people everywhere. I am not sure how they got in the house until I spy Meg in the kitchen sipping coffee. She looks up from her coffee and blows me a kiss. She holds up her phone, indicating she's on a call and will be up soon. A team from the supply company was on the porch arranging chairs, the runner, and decorating. A catering group had just arrived to begin prep.

I squeeze between them to grab our coffees before they get too busy. Sadly, it may be a one-cup day. The hair and make-up duo we've hired for the day will be here at 9 a.m. I get busy helping Hattie and the dogs get their start for the day to avoid getting behind.

When the front door swings open, I smell coffee and breakfast. Hattie and I groan with relief that Erin and the girls planned ahead. They've brought more than we need and I am so happy to see it. Erin smiles and says, "I figured it might be a little busy here." She gestures around her to all of the people in motion. There must now be at least fifteen people moving in and out of the house. Bless her for planning on a day when I couldn't!

Seeing all the activity is stressing me out. Kayla and Lauren spin me around and up the stairs, pushing me back to the landing. Surf and Erin help Hattie slowly ascend behind us. All of us are loaded with breakfast goods, and we can't wait to dig in.

Shortly after we had inhaled our breakfast, our wedding day transformations began. Our local salon's hair and makeup team are miracle workers, and I need it after a mostly sleepless night. I was too keyed up, tossing and turning throughout the night, checking my phone for the time. With each check, I calculated how long before my alarm went off. I could also hear Hattie up and down a few times. Despite regaining most of her strength, she still makes me nervous when she's up alone. Did not make for a restful night. The bags under my eyes display that for all my guests to witness.

I'd managed to sneak in a prep session with the team two weeks ago, so we know exactly what the plan is for me. Everyone else shares inspiration pictures of hair and makeup, all realistic and ideally suited to them. Our glam squad gets to work while we pop a cork to make peach bellinis. Why not celebrate this early on a Saturday?

Around 1 p.m., we are nearly done, and I hear Cal's rumbling voice ask, "Are y'all decent?" with a chuckle. He came to check on us and brought a charcuterie plate with mini-pecan pies courtesy of Sarah. At this point, my excitement has taken over, and the best I can do is nibble on cheese and a few grapes. Hattie and Erin both encourage me to eat. But I feel incapable.

I'm not nervous in the "I don't want to marry Max" way, more in the "everyone will be watching us" way. Getting married and saying the vows we wrote for each other is so personal. We've invited so few for the ceremony, and at this moment, there are still too many. How can I share the way I feel about Max with everyone watching?

I start to feel cold, sweaty, hot, and dizzy. Hattie comes to sit next to me. Without a word, she rests her hand over mine. I hear her low humming—an unnamed melody from my childhood and hers. When I was young and too overcome to share what I thought or felt, we would sit like this. She would wait until I was ready. As we sit, and she hums while resting next to me, my heart rate begins to slow. The tightness in my chest eases. I can do this.

The guests at the wedding are our family and closest friends, they're all well aware of how much Max and I care for one another. Even if they haven't heard us say it aloud. I turn my hand over and lace my fingers through Hattie's. She squeezes my fingers and continues humming softly. I close my eyes and enjoy the comfort of having her with me. In the back of my mind is the voice telling me these moments will be few. Instead of hearing it, I focus on Hattie's song and how much love I feel in this space. Whether anyone in the room has noticed or not, I don't know. This was one of those special memories I will tuck away.

Cal catches us up on the progress Max and the guys have made. All had eaten and showered, and they walked by the beach and sat down and had coffee when he left. The only tasks left were getting dressed and driving over to the house. It's such a different pace than our day!

He'll take our dogs over to spend the rest of the evening with theirs, and a dog sitter will hang out with them until everyone is home. Before leaving, Cal slips a thin box from his jacket pocket and says, "A gift from your husband." He gives me a hug and a peck on the cheek. I withdraw a thin diamond bracelet from the box; in the center are the initials "G & M." He helps me clasp it on my wrist. It catches the light, sparkling in the sun. Everyone gathers round to take a peek, and all of us are delighted by the bracelet. Kayla teases Cal that Eddie should take note of it for an upcoming gift. After a round of goodbyes, Cal makes his way to gather the dogs with Erin's assistance. She's decided to dress at home and arrive at the ceremony with him.

Before the photographer arrives, Hattie and I prepare my dress and the bridesmaids. She's opted out of the getting ready shots, it's too hard for her. She prefers to save her strength for the evening ahead. I help her get ready and sit to rest for a while. She decides to close her eyes for a moment and is asleep within minutes. I'm glad she'll be able to rest for a while.

All too soon, we're taking the required pre-ceremony photos. Once we're all dressed, it is time for us to gather for bridal party shots and my pictures with Hattie. The hours before the wedding blitz past. Meg and Sarah tap on the door with sweet treats and champagne to signal it is almost time. By now, I am hungry and take some of the snacks they've delivered. We hear the buzz of guests arriving, then Max, the groomsman, and his parents. Before leaving, Meg and Sarah escort Hattie downstairs. She decided it is easier for her to be seated before I walk out.

The ceremony begins right on time. Max's parents walk down the aisle first and take their seats in the front row. Hattie should already be in her seat, ready to give me away. I can't quite see her and wish that I could. There is a solid pull to stand on my tiptoes and try to find her. But, I ultimately decided that would appear childish and wait.

The music begins with an instrumental piece that took us far too long to select. Each of Max's siblings prepares to walk in turn. Surf and Jimmy, Lauren and Max's friend Graham, Eddie, and Kayla, with baby

Annabelle between them. They all look so lovely walking down the printed carpet.

When the music changes, it's my turn. I step to the doorway, drawing a deep, centering breath. To calm myself, I take in the transformation of the porch. The runner has been placed, and chairs are arranged in rows of four with camellias and ivy on the ends. Our handmade arch at the front, draped in tulle with twinkling lights, strands of ivy are woven with camellias and baby's breath. Candles on stands light all around the porch, creating a beautiful glow in the late afternoon light. It looks absolutely magical.

All eyes turn to me, and I seek out Max. He locks onto my gaze, and a smile lights up his face, dimples deeper than ever. He's devastatingly handsome in his deep blue tux with a crisp white shirt. He maintains a tan all year from being out on the water, and it contrasts with his shirt. I return his beaming smile and pause before stepping out on my own. My heart flutters wildly in my chest, and I feel lightheaded. The love I feel pouring out of Max bolsters my confidence. The nerves I felt seconds ago fade away.

As I take the first step, a small, warm hand glides into the crook of my arm. I gasp with delight when I see Hattie by my side. Tears sting my eyes and flow freely from her own. She's been there all my life, and on my most significant day, she is here despite everything. She pats my arm and whispers, "Your husband is waiting." We chuckle softly and then match our steps to the music, making our way to Max.

Writing our vows was a fun and emotional experience. Sharing what we want to say, making it loving and humorous while staying dignified, was no small task. The moment arrives when we exchange vows, and our hands and voices shake. The officiant calls on Max to begin, and I am secretly grateful (maybe not so secretly) that he has to start us off.

"Greer, standing here with you today feels like a dream come true. From childhood friends to husband and wife, our lives have not turned out like we'd pictured. Every day with you fills my heart with joy and happiness that I did not expect and cannot imagine life without. I am inspired by your gratitude, kindness, and warmth. I promise to care for you and stand by you each day. To be your anchor and strength, a shelter from the storms that will come our way. I cannot wait to see what life holds for us, and I vow to be at your side for each moment. I choose you, today, tomorrow, forever." By the time he finishes, there is not a dry eye on the porch, and I am trying to frantically wipe away the tears falling. Max reaches into his pocket, withdraws a handkerchief, and gently dabs my tears away. He rests his hand on my cheek for the briefest second. We both give a nod, and he winks. The officiant asks me if I'm ready to begin. I smile and nod happily. Really and truly ready.

"Max, growing up together, I never would have imagined this day. My friend, my confidant, and now you're my husband. The joy and gratitude I feel at becoming your wife is overwhelming. You're the safe harbor in those rough seas, a steady place. I promise to be the same for you—a place of warmth, love, and safety. There's a home in my heart that you will always have. As we walk, or sail, through life together, I vow to support you and cherish those bonds of love we share. I am so glad you've chosen me, and I can't wait to begin our life together."

The officiant pronounces us husband and wife, and Max sweeps me off my feet in a dramatic kiss to the delight of our guests. I cannot believe I am now Mrs. Maxwell Vaughn! Now we party.

Chapter Seventeen

-Hattie-

What a stunning wedding! Greer and Max could have been a couple from a magazine. Her petite light coloring in ivory, contrasting with his large frame and dark coloring in deep blue. The beading on the lace bodice of her dress sparkled in the afternoon light and later in the candles. We all nearly swooned when he dipped her for their first kiss as man and wife. It was like a scene from a movie and from the expression on her face, completely unrehearsed.

The wedding party wore sage and blue with baby Annabelle in a tiny ivory dress. She looked like a little doll. Kayla's baby bump was mostly hidden by the folds of her dress, but it won't be long until their sweet new addition joins the family. Us old folks even wore matching sage and navy colors to complement the wedding party. Erin and I had a ball finding dresses for the wedding. We felt young and old searching for the right ones in the "mother of the bride" sections in the bridal boutiques. Erin wore an off-the-shoulder navy sheath dress with beading on the bodice that trailed off near the hips. I opted for a Greek goddess–inspired sage dress with flowing fabric that fanned when I walked. Cal was as handsome as ever in his tux and boutonnieres. He gallantly escorted Erin and I into the reception.

Camellias and ivy dripped from bouquets, corsages, boutonnieres, and garlands. By the ceremony's conclusion, the sun was setting, and all of the candles and twinkle lights gave off the most romantic glow. I had no idea the porch could look so good! I could not have asked for a more picturesque evening.

We sent Max and Greer off on their two-week honeymoon that night. She doesn't know, but he's taking her to a resort in Jamaica that she's been drooling over online. While they're away, Lauren has graciously volunteered to be my roommate and babysitter (my phrase, no one else's). She works mainly from home doing marketing and billing for the family businesses, putting those degrees to work. She'll be able to use Greer's old office.

On that front, Greer officially gave notice to her company that she won't be returning. With my health and getting married, she has a very full plate and decided she is happy with her life as is—no need to complicate or add stress. I have to say, I am so proud of her. That job was a bright spot for years, and then suddenly wasn't. In my opinion, it takes a lot to realize when something is no longer serving you and to move on.

Lauren and I are taking breaks from cooking for the next two weeks. We've planned to eat through the freezer and order out for other nights. Greer loves to cook and has stocked the freezer with so many different meals that we could eat from there for months. Lauren isn't big on cooking to start. I have lost my passion for it. Standing in the kitchen takes too much out of me. Tonight, we feast on Caesar salads and pizza from our local favorite, Capio's. It's not a bad kick-off meal if you ask us.

Cold weather has moved in this week. Sylvie and Ben tease me relentlessly for my use of "cold." Having moved from the northeast to Florida and now here, our version of winter weather is blissful for them. The change in temperatures has me moving slower and coughing more.

All the wedding festivities took more out of me than I'll ever admit out loud, which isn't helping any. I am moving like a woman several decades older than my actual age. I am confident this isn't precisely what Lauren thought she was signing up for when she agreed to spend the time with me. But at least we've got the cozy fireplace, lots of good wine, and tasty food to get us through the rough patches. The forecast calls for a few frigid nights ahead, so we will batten down the hatches and bring in extra logs. We'll be just fine.

–Greer–

We are in a literal paradise. I can see why Max kept this a secret. I've been dreaming of coming here, but I absolutely would have tried to talk him out of this. The resort is unreal, with a room that opens onto a patio and our own small pool. We're surrounded by lush vegetation and gorgeous tropical flowers. I cannot even begin to describe the quality of the food appropriately. There's a chef on site who makes lunch and dinner each day, incorporating local flavors. On Friday night, we had slow-roasted pork wrapped in banana leaves, sticky rice, and a mango side dish that was sweeter than honey. I'll never look at pork the same again.

Tomorrow, we are back to reality, and while I'm not sad to go home, I am sorry to give up having my husband all to myself and no responsibility. We linger in bed every morning, getting up only when we want or when the pull for coffee is stronger than for one another. The rest of the day is spent relaxing.

I read, and Max sketches or paints. I surprised him with a small watercolor set, and he's used it daily. We swim in the warm salty water and then bake on the sand, we take long romantic walks, soak in the hot tub, swing in the hammock in the salty sea air. Spending two weeks in paradise with my dreamy husband is more than I could have imagined. This is what honeymoon fantasies are made of, but you never think it will happen.

On our final night, we slowly pack our belongings and gifts and prepare to say goodbye to this slice of paradise. Max rolls his small paintings into tight bundles and places them carefully into his carry-on. We discuss where we'll hang them when the house is finished. I'm picturing us talking about the memories they'll call up for decades. Thinking of our home and the progress to be made makes me a teeny bit antsy to get home.

I call Hattie to give her updated arrival times to the airport and the house. I switch to video and show her our patio and the beach in the distance. She's as delighted with it as we've been and says the pictures we have sent didn't do it justice. In all fairness, she had forbidden me to call. Tonight, I broke her rule and was shocked when she answered.

Throughout the call, I notice she was more short of breath than usual and seemed to cough after longer sentences. When I ask, she chalks it up to the weather and talks about the temperature and dampness. Her color looks off again. It's not a color that I can describe accurately from a video call. Max gestures to me from off-camera, making a circular motion around his face and a quizzical expression. I nod as he mouths, "Her color is off." This has historically not been good. We chat for a little longer until a coughing spell cuts the call short. Lauren entered the room to check on her as Hattie hangs up. As if reading my mind, Max says, "I'm calling Mom."

Erin answers after a few rings, cheerful and sur-prised to hear from us. We feel guilty that we haven't called yet. To relieve some of that, we flip the phone around and give a tour of the room and patio, showing the moon over the beach. Max asks how things have been over the last few weeks. Erin also mentions the chilly, damp weather and hopes we packed sweaters or coats to wear once we land. We assure her we have. Then I say that Hattie mentioned the weather change and that it has affected her somewhat. Erin pauses and draws a steadying breath; she looks over the top of her phone for a second. Cal says something inaudible. Erin returns to her phone and apologizes for not talking with us sooner.

"It's been your honeymoon, and I didn't want to spoil it or bring you down," she hesitantly states. Neither of us speaks while we wait for her to continue. Erin clearly needs a moment. "This has not been a good week for Hattie. Cal and I took her to the ER two nights ago for an evaluation. The doctor diagnosed an early pneumonia. It was Dr. Ingles who saw her again. He said it was very early, and she is safe to be treated at home. The home health team decided to increase her care to be safe. There's a nurse and Lauren at the house with her now. Lauren is there mostly for comfort and the dogs. She felt way out of her league with the breathing treatments and new medications added in."

My mind goes completely blank for a second, and I feel anxious and calm at the same time. How am I so far away when she's sick? There are dozens of thoughts flying around in my head, but I can't seem to catch one to make it into a logical statement or question. Obviously, if Hattie had been dramatically ill, they would have had us come home. This is not our first rodeo with hospitalizations.

Max speaks first, asking about the plan and recovery times. Erin fills us in by saying that Dr. Ingles believes Hattie could have picked it up anywhere, at any time. She'd started returning to her ladies' meetings at the library on Tuesdays and isn't sure if she got it there or from a doctor's appointment. With an intense course of two antibiotics, cough medications, breathing treatments, and her existing oxygen, the team is hopeful she'll be feeling better within a week.

Her primary care and specialists are involved. She has appointments sprinkled throughout the next several days and which are now shared via email to add to our calendars. She sends over the new medication lists and schedules. We mention the coughing spell that ended our call and her poor coloring before this. Erin frowns and looks concerned. She'd visited Hattie earlier in the day and she was feeling better and not coughing.

In the interim, a rainstorm moved in, bringing the temperatures down to nearly freezing again. Erin and Cal talk quickly, then tell us they'd better go over to check on Hattie and Lauren. Both may be stressed by the situation even though the homecare nurse is there. They ring off, promising to keep us updated. We'll call again from the airport tomorrow morning.

What should have been a sweet and relaxing final night has now turned into a night filled with anxiety and planning for our return home. We pack quickly. We decide to walk on the beach to tire ourselves out and eliminate some of our nervous energy. Max mixes two drinks from the bar in our room, and we set out for our final moonlit stroll on the beach.

The waves seem louder and closer than on previous nights. Their repetitive thunderous crashing is sooth-ing. I feel small, but it gives me perspective. This might all seem overwhelming at the moment, but we'll get through it. Max slips his hand into mine and squeezes. I lace my fingers with him while we walk along in silence. As we move through the cool sand, dodging small crabs, the warm water splashing our feet and legs, I soak in the moment. I hear Hattie's voice, reminding me to find gratitude.

I softly clear my throat and am about to speak when Max says, "Looking back on this week and the last few months. There have been so many unforeseeable changes, challenges, blessings, and moments of happiness. A lesson I've learned from you and Hattie is to think about all of it. Not just in single moments. For that, I am immensely grateful. For you, her, and the lessons we're learning together." I throw my arm around his waist as we continue our walk back. This was what we needed. A walk to give us time to reset and take on whatever is coming next. Tonight, we'll spend the final night of our honeymoon in paradise, and then we'll tackle the rest together.

Erin calls just before bed. Hattie's cough improved with a double breathing treatment. While still pale, the dusky blueness around her lips is gone, too. She and Cal have opted to spend the day with Hattie. The nurse is there and has checked her over before bed. A Nurse Practitioner from the home care company is coming in the morning to review the medications and treatment plans. Lauren has a full day of meetings, so it makes sense for them to stick around. Knowing Hattie has so much support and has improved since the call; we turn into bed. We drift off with the patio doors open, listening to the crashing waves and light rain—a perfect lullaby in paradise.

Sunshine and the call of birds awaken us before the alarm. Not the worst wakeup ever. Coffee is delivered to our room each morning just before we wake up. We hear the light knock on the door, and I offer to get it. Max is already starting to sit up, "You stay there and enjoy for another minute. I'll bring it to you."

I smile as he pads away to the hotel room door, wrapped in one of the terry-cloth robes. While he's up, I rearrange our pillows so we can savor our coffee. My phone dings, and I commit to ignoring it until we are at least a cup deep. The coffee here is meant to be savored, not gulped in between messages and emails.

Max returns with a tray laden with coffee, pastries, and a stunning tropical floral arrangement—a gift on our last day from the hotel. We inhale the sweetness of the flowers and place them at the bedside, unsure how we'll get any of them home. I pour two steaming cups of coffee, and Max plates the pastries. We take the first several sips black to enjoy the flavor and smooth texture of the brew. I then add a splash of cream to each and a sprinkle of sugar for Max.

"I'm gonna miss this," I murmur.

"The resort?" he asks.

"Yes, but I meant the coffee," I say as I take another sip of the deliciously hot coffee. He softly chuckles and nods his head.

Coffee and pastries consumed. Finally, I turn to check my phone which has been making intermittent buzzing and pinging sounds. None of which I was all that interested in, they weren't text or phone call alerts. So, it had nothing to

do with Hattie. Flipping my phone over, I groan loudly.

"A four-hour delay....." I sigh and hold the airline app up for Max to see. He matches my groan and flops his head back.

Hours later, at the airport, we text Hattie to check in, letting her know our boarding and arrival times. I send a photo of us blowing her a kiss. With the time change to our flight, it is late for her. We called briefly when we left the hotel, but she was already in bed and half asleep. Despite the late hour, the messages are marked as "read," and Hattie loves them both, sending back, "*See you soon, sweets*" with a heart emoji. I send back, "*You should be sleeping,*" with a crazy-eyed emoji. Hattie sends back a series of laughing faces and tears. She must be in that exhausted and too tired to sleep phase. I tell her sweet dreams, how much we love her, and will see her soon. With a *"nighty-night,"* she hopefully can sleep for the night.

Chapter Eighteen

♥

That was the longest flight ever, we were tossed around for nearly the entire five hours. It was rocky from takeoff to touch down. Arriving in Jacksonville, it was pouring rain and almost thirty degrees colder than we'd been for two weeks. My teeth began chattering the moment we left the terminal. We rush to start the heat in the truck and get out of the ice-cold rain.

"My God, no wonder Hattie ended up sick!" I exclaim, rubbing my hands together.

Neither of us can remember being this cold in early January. Max starts the truck, and we celebrate the feeling of heated seats while we search for the missing parking ticket. The heat was finally blasting, and GPS started. We were ready to get on the road to home. I text the group to announce our safe arrival and to give an estimated time for us to be at the house. Most of the family will be up by now or very shortly, so I don't worry about waking them. No one responds, but we aren't super concerned. They at least know we are back.

We debate stopping for coffee, but land on waiting to share the coffee we've brought back with Hattie and whomever is at the house. To keep ourselves awake, we rehash some of our favorite memories of the trip. The time passes in a flash, and we're soon in the circular drive in front of the house.

All seems quiet, with only a few lights on. Erin's SUV is parked in front, Lauren's car is off to the side, and one I don't recognize parked on the street. I assume it belongs to the home care nurse who has been staying at the house.

Thankfully, the rain has slowed from an all-out downpour to a drizzle as we pull to a stop. Max and I quickly grab our bags and rush to the front door. I'm fumbling with my keys wishing I'd thought to get them out before we exited the truck. I finally find the right one and triumphantly hold it up to Max. As I slide it into the lock, the door opens from inside, confusing us both for a second. I hadn't even turned the knob.

From the look on Erin's face, I know. My bags fall to the ground, and I rush past her into Hattie's bedroom. "Hattie?" my voice is thick, sounding nearly strangled. Cal and Lauren are sitting at the foot of her bed. The nurse is kneeling beside her, holding her hand. The dogs are scattered throughout the room, and Sandie is lying protectively, facing the doorway. She whines softly when I enter.

I slowly walk to the right side of the bed, and the nurse stands as I approach. Her empathetic gaze is heartbreaking. I wish I could do more than glance at her, but it's all I can do. I drop to my knees and grab her hand. I rub it between mine, hers is too cool and limp. Maybe I can bring some warmth back to her? This isn't real; I'd only spoken to her a few hours ago; we'd texted right before bed.

"Hattie, please......" I beg, leaning forward to rest my head against her frail shoulder. There's no soothing hand to pat my head, no heartbeat echoing in her chest to calm me—only crushing silence. Hattie is so still and small. A grief-stricken, choking sob escapes me. I know we've reached the end, but I cannot bear it at this moment.

A solid, warm hand rests on my shoulder. Max. He whispers, "Greer..." and I shake my head. I can't hear the next part of what he has to say, it will be too much. I reach up and grab his hand tightly, clinging to him like a lifeline. I hear rustling and shuffling as the family change positions in the room, then muted voices from the kitchen. The others have left us here with Hattie. Her ever-present dogs stay with her. They take their spots around the edges of her bed. Intermittent soft whines escape but none will leave the room. All facing out toward the door, like they're watching over her. That only adds to the hurt. People say we don't deserve the love dogs give, but she did.

Max positions me into a chair and off the floor, pressing a cup of hot tea into my freezing hands. He covers my lap with a blanket. Without asking, he spreads a throw over Hattie. He knows that in my mind, however senseless, I am still concerned that she's cold. The rain continues to pour outside, thunder rattles the windows, and lightning sends flashes into the room. I don't know how long we sat there, the three of us. Erin enters quietly and beckons Max into the hallway. On his return, he crouches before me, taking my empty tea mug, which I have no memory of drinking.

"Greer, baby, the funeral home will be here in a few minutes. It's time to start getting ready."

I'm startled that they've been notified. Of course, they have, but how did we know who to call and who made the call? We need to get things ready to take and the paperwork started. Nothing is ready. I haven't seen the paperwork in months. There has to be something we need to do. I start to jump up from my chair. Max must see the panicked expression begin to take over, and he puts a calming hand on my leg.

"Hattie had put the arrangements in place. She'd given it to the home healthcare company to make sure it would all be handled. Mom and the nurse have been on the phone with them and set it up." I sag with relief.

I won't have to make the calls and say any of this out loud yet. The tears flow in steady streams, my shirt front is soaking wet. When I try to stand, my legs shake. Max pulls me into him as we walk to Hattie's bed. The entire family, with Meg, Sylvie, and Ben, join us as we say our final goodbyes. We take our turns and leave the room one by one to wait in the kitchen.

We're seated around the table, tightly packed in. A fire roars in the living room, and the house feels warmer than it has been all day. The storms have finally stopped, replaced by a soft, steady rain. Tumblers of whiskey have replaced tea mugs. Finally, feeling strong enough, I ask what happened.

Erin swirls the whiskey in her tumbler and says, "I'm not really sure. The nurse suspects another heart attack in her sleep. We'd come over after we talked last night. The nurse had her breathing treatment in progress. Afterward, we watched a movie. She was feeling better, maybe a little keyed up from the medicine but said her breathing was better, and was not coughing as much. I helped her get settled in for the night around 11:30, then Cal and I went up to bed. I checked on her around 3 am, and she was sleeping peacefully; her breathing was nice and regular. I even checked her oxygen saturation, and it was within the limits the doctor gave us. Not coughing at all," Erin pauses to wipe her eyes and blow her nose. Cal rubs her back gently to support her. She takes a few shuddering breaths and continues, "We woke up right before you texted, and I came down to let the dogs out and make coffee. I knocked, and she didn't answer. I thought she must have been sleeping still after her late night. So, I just put the dogs out quietly. When I brought in her coffee..." Erin begins sobbing and falls onto Cal's shoulder. She isn't able to continue, sobs overtake her.

He picks up the story from here, "When Erin brought in the coffee, she immediately knew something was wrong and shouted for help. The nurse and I came in, and we both knew that Hattie had passed. We had been in with her for about 10 minutes when you arrived. We are so sorry, sweetie. If there was any way we would have known or any hints, we would have taken her to the hospital the night before." Cal, too, becomes choked up. He and Erin sit with their arms around one another.

I rush over and sit with them, wrapping my arms around both of them. This is not their fault, and I need them to know that. Nothing could have prevented this, most likely not even if Hattie had been in the hospital. Her heart couldn't hold out anymore. It had only been a matter of time.

Hattie's funeral was held on the following Tuesday. The funeral home ran out of seating, and folks stood in the entryway. She was as loved in death as she was in life. Joel and Janine were even able to make it in from Idaho. We buried her between Davis and Mama in the Thatcher family plot. It was fitting that on the day of her funeral, the sun was shining, and it was unseasonably warm. It felt like the sun was out for her.

After the funeral, Max and I come back to Davis and Hattie's big old house. We'll always think of it as their house. In honor of Hattie, we finally brewed a pot of the coffee we'd brought her from Jamaica. As it was finishing, the doorbell rang. While the dogs, including Brady, swirled around me, I hurried off to answer.

On the front porch, I found Erin, Cal, and Lauren with a plate full of snacks and a cooler of steaks for the grill. Smiling, I usher them in. From the backyard, I hear Max talking and wonder who it could be. We exit to find Meg, her new beau, and the twins with fresh bread, cookies, sweet tea, and cold wine. A cheer arises—this is starting to feel like a porch party. I mention that I should call Sylvie, and the doorbell rings again.

Amidst raised eyebrows and "who could that be?" Max heads to the door and returns with Sylvie, Ben, Surf, and Jimmy. All loaded with plates and platters of delicious food. The dogs run in circles in the yard, barking and playing. Happy chaos reigns down. We quickly drag out the tables, chairs, and dinnerware. This feels like the right way to celebrate Hattie's life. Together in her favorite place, with her favorite people.

Epilogue

♥

Three years later

Sitting on my front porch, listening to the water lap the dock, my thoughts turn to Hattie—her love of sun, water, and dogs. Max and I finished our little cottage a year after Hattie passed. While she didn't get to see the house to completion, I'm so happy we got to bring her here and share our dreams of it with her.

Max built his studio and paints almost daily, sharing scenes of our beloved Georgia coast with people all over the world. Paintings from our honeymoon hang inside our home and in Hattie's. He brings to life the beauty around him. I think Hattie would genuinely appreciate that. He runs fishing charters a few times a month, but mostly, he paints.

Today, I watched our daughter play in the front yard with the dogs and thought how much she would love to see this and her. Our daughter is her father's spitting image but reminds us so much of Hattie. Feisty, funny, and loves to be outside. She'll be two in a couple of weeks and is in awe of everything in the world around her. She's surrounded by a family that loves her deeply and will support her for life. We haven't told anyone, but baby number two is on the way. He'll be here in 6 short months.

Eddie and Kayla welcomed a son, James Calvin Vaughn, a few months after our wedding and are currently expecting baby number three! They've taken on more of the construction business as Cal approaches retirement. Every year, they get busier and busier.

Jimmy and Surf haven't started a family but recently moved back to Georgia. Jimmy is done with the offshore diving life and now works for a Conservation team focused on sea life in our coastal waters. He and Surf spend most of their days together underwater and are as happy as they could ever be.

Lauren has taken on a major role in running the café and is now engaged to Graham, Max's friend. They met at our wedding. She lives in a house that she bought from Max and I. It was one of the rental properties that Hattie and Davis turned over to us.

Meg has remarried the beau she introduced us all to at the wedding. He is an accountant who relocated here from D.C. following his divorce several years ago. The twins adore him, and all are happy. The twins head to college in the fall. Each to their own schools, nowhere near one another. That was a tough one for Meg. She's adjusting to the idea of her babies becoming independent.

Erin and Cal are inching toward retirement. They're finally owning up to being sixty and said they've worked hard and are ready to turn it over to the kids. We all have a hand in the business as they get ready to launch. Their first big trip is to Hawaii with no kids or grandkids in 2 months. They're gathering tips on grandparenting from Sylvie and Ben.

Sylvie and Ben have had six more grandchildren join the ranks and are exhausted from trips up and down the coast. They said they didn't know it would be this tiring, but they love it! The shop has expanded into the location next door, and they've hired a manager to give them more free time for travel. Aubrey does a great job and lets them focus on other things.

Each year on the anniversary of Hattie's death, we gather for a porch party, in her honor. She taught me many lessons. The most important for me is that family is not always blood, and to find something to be grateful for every day. I found my family through friendship and marriage. Every day, I find something I can find joy in, even on the bad days. It makes life more enjoyable, and for that, I am immensely grateful.

About the author

Kate Montgomery is a fiction writer living in Georgia with her family and pets. A nature enthusiast, she enjoys spending time outdoors, drawing inspiration from the beauty around her. Her family and faith are important parts of her life, and she brings those values into her writing.